Julie Bozza

The Thousand Smiles of Nicholas Goring

LIBRAtiger

Published by LIBRAtiger 2018

ISBN: 978-1-925869-20-0

First published by Manifold Press 2014

Text: © Julie Bozza 2018
Proof–reading and line editing: F.M. Parkinson
Editor: Fiona Pickles of Manifold Press
Print format: © Julie Bozza 2018
Set in Adobe Caslon Pro and Adobe Gothic

Cover design: © Gayna Murphy of Mubu Design | mubudesign.com

libra-tiger.com | juliebozza.com

Acknowledgement

For one last time, I humbly hope for the reader's tolerance. Part of this story deals with things that some will say don't concern me. But I do so with nothing in my heart but a love of and a wish for interdependence between all our peoples – and for that perhaps any infelicities will be forgiven.

Dedication

With thanks to everyone who has accompanied Dave and Nicholas on their journey.

one

"So," said Denise, "you're seven years married. Are you feeling the itch yet?"

Dave scowled over his mug of coffee. "No," was his honest response. But then he cast her a doubting look. "I always thought that was kind of a, uh – *gross* way to put it. I mean, if you're married, you shouldn't be out there catching the nasty kind of things that make you itch. Right?"

Denise laughed. "True. And if you're not feeling the urge to stray, Davey, then I guess all is well in Goring Taylor Land."

"Everything's fine with me and Nicholas, yeah." He considered her for a long moment, wondering what she was driving at. "But you know I'm the loyal sort. I wouldn't 'stray' even if things weren't fine."

"I know that, Davey," she offered reassuringly. She took a mouthful of her coffee, and they both stared contemplatively out beyond the backyard.

It was a warm winter's day in Brisbane, and the French windows were open to let in the fresh air. Denise and Vittorio's house was on a bit of a hill, so there was a view over the back fence of a wide stretch of rooftops and trees, and the cluster of taller buildings in the city centre, and then beyond that a blue haze which Dave could sometimes convince himself was the ocean. Dave squinted, adjusted his new glasses on his nose, and tried to judge how much further he could see now … Well, the high-rises were certainly more sharply delineated, but he figured the ocean view was still more wishful thinking than not.

"How are you finding them?" Denise asked, lifting her chin to indicate the glasses. "Getting used to wearing them all day?"

"Yeah, they're fine." He added, "It's only the right eye that's short-sighted, you know. The left eye's spot on."

She snorted. "Oh, as long as you're only half defective, that's all right, then."

"Thanks!"

"Nah …" Denise turned in her chair to consider him again. "You're looking good, Davey. Those frames suit you. Very … I dunno. Somewhere between trendy and sophisticated."

"Thanks."

"Definitely sexy," she said –

– and his cheeks went pink, he just knew it. Dave stared studiously at his coffee mug on the table before him, and feebly offered his thanks yet again. It still mattered to him, just a little bit – even after all these years – that Denny might think him handsome. "Um …" He cleared his throat, and sought to change the subject. "Vittorio's at work, then?"

"Yes. And Nicholas is at uni?"

"Yes." He didn't dare look at her. They both knew where their husbands were. Somehow that hadn't changed the subject at all, but only intensified it.

Denise commented rather pointedly, "Zoe and Bethan are at school until three …"

A silence stretched.

"Um …" Then finally Dave dared to glance at her, and saw she was brimming over with mirth. He guffawed as she burst out laughing. "God!" he managed. "You had me thinking *you* were the one feeling an itch!"

"Nah … All's well in Agostini Land, too."

"Excellent."

They sat there for a while, drinking their coffee. Then Denise observed, "You *are* looking good, though, Dave. You always did, of course, but I have to say you're maturing very nicely indeed."

And he was blushing again. "God's sake, Denny," he grumbled. "What on Earth are you going on about?"

"I was just thinking … If you want to distract young Robin from Nicholas, that's certainly one way to go about it."

It was Dave's turn to snort. "I shouldn't think he'll ever get over Nicholas, not really … But after all this time … I mean, it'll have mellowed a bit, don't you reckon?"

"Ha! How old is he? Seventeen, eighteen?"

"Eighteen."

"Like *anything* feels mellow at that age – let alone love!"

Dave sighed, remembering his own devotion to Denise during his teens, thinking of Nicholas's steadfast passion for Frank Brambell, the Goring family chauffeur. If Nicholas's nephew Robin was made of the same stuff, then there could be some shoal-filled waters to navigate during the next three months. "I'm sure it'll be fine," Dave said, not knowing whom he was trying to convince. "They've both been looking forward to this for, like, eighteen months or whatever. Since we went over there, two Christmases ago."

"He's flying in tomorrow, isn't he?"

"Yes, early start in the morning to go pick him up."

"Well, bring him over to dinner whenever suits – you know, once he's over the jet lag. I know you'll be wanting to head off to the waterhole, but it'd be good to see him again."

"Thanks, Denny." He smiled at her fondly, and they talked about matters less fundamental than love until it was finally time for Dave to mosey on home … Before he quite left, though – before he'd opened the front screen-door – Dave turned and asked, "Things are really okay?"

"Course they are, Davey."

"No, uh – no nine-year itches for you?"

"Not even a twitch."

He leaned in to press an affectionate kiss to her cheek – and she took the opportunity to grab him in a rare shoulder-cracking hug. "I'm glad," he said, once she'd let him go again.

And she wrinkled her nose at him with a loving grin. "Me, too. See ya, mate."

"See ya, Denny." And he finally let himself out, and walked home.

When Nicholas got home from uni that evening, he announced that he didn't want much to eat for dinner. Dave examined him with an anxious gaze, looking for any signs of stress or pain. But Nicholas seemed no worse than a little tired, which was only to be expected at the end of a full working day – and a bright glance from under his brow soon convinced Dave that Nicholas was in fact feeling very well indeed. With a wink, Nicholas explained, "It'll be my last chance for a while to provoke you into making some noise …"

Dave smiled, and returned his attention to the tomatoes he was chopping for the salad.

"I can't wait to see Robin again," Nicholas continued, coming over to press a kiss to Dave's nape and steal a slice of tomato from the chopping board, "but there's no denying a long-term house guest is going to prove damned inconvenient at times."

"You know you'll love having him here."

Nicholas murmured an agreement, before almost literally poking his nose into the salad bowl. "Your world-famous chicken and new potato salad … ? Well, I was serious, you know. How about we have half now, and save the rest for after? I'm sure I can work us hard enough to earn a midnight snack."

"Always happy to rise to a challenge …" Dave replied as smoothly as he could.

"Mmm …" Nicholas's hand lowered again – but this time he boldly and unerringly cupped Dave's tackle through his jeans, and gave it an encouraging jostle. "Hold that thought! I'm just going to get changed."

Dave managed to touch a fleeting kiss to Nicholas's cheek even as he turned away, and then Dave had the chance to admire that fine tall figure walking out of the kitchen and into the hall. Nicholas always insisted on wearing a suit to work, though it wasn't at all necessary – but Dave couldn't deny the man looked absolutely gorgeous in suits. That day's effort was a dark blue, perfectly tailored to Nicholas's slim waist and strong shoulders.

Within a few minutes, Dave had finished preparing the salad, and dished out half of it into pasta bowls. He was covering the remaining salad with Glad Wrap prior to putting it in the fridge, when Nicholas reappeared – transformed into something more like a regular Aussie in a t-shirt and worn jeans, barefoot, and with his dark hair mussed. Nicholas grinned at him, and they exchanged a kiss full of promise before taking their dinner through to the lounge, and eating with Splayds while watching the ABC TV news.

Not that they paid much attention to the news; they sat there together in comfortable silence, or exchanged quiet comments and questions about their days. Nicholas had some kind of official affiliation with the university which enabled him to pursue his research; Dave wasn't sure exactly how it all worked, but Nicholas went in for at least one full day each week, and often more. Nicholas also did some teaching there, though right from the start he'd negotiated that being on a fairly casual basis, because he liked to be free to join Dave on his trips to the Outback. Not that Nicholas wanted to be included on every trip, whether it was with clients or even when Dave went to sing the Dreamtime songs with Charlie at the waterhole – but Nicholas liked it to be his own decision and, as he said, he could always justify any trip with research.

After they'd eaten the salad, Nicholas sat back – and Dave remembered to take his glasses off before being welcomed into the man's arms. Nicholas held him there warm and safe, pressing lazy kisses to his hair and stroking at his arms and chest and stomach, lulling him into a luxurious kind of comfort … The TV burbled on until Nicholas reached for the remote and turned it off, and then the cosy silence was free to well between them. Eventually Nicholas tucked his head in beside Dave's, and murmured in his ear, "Anything in particular you feel like doing tonight … ? Or anything you *don't* feel like doing?"

"Anything," Dave echoed – knowing very well that Nicholas would respect his wishes, but also trusting that whatever Nicholas wanted to do would be absolutely fine by him. "You're the creative one," he added, twisting a little to flash his lover a grin.

Nicholas laughed under his breath. "Well … tonight I feel like … going all out. Doing a bit of everything. Is that all right?"

"*Hell*, yes," Dave whispered fervently.

"And I want … I want you to tell me how it feels."

Dave cast him a doubtful look.

"You know, just … make a bit of noise. That's all."

"I can do that," said Dave, relaxing again. He'd long ago learned how a throaty guttural groan could add to the joy felt by his other senses, and he suspected he probably made plenty of other kinds of sounds, too, when in the heart of it.

"All right, then …" After a moment, Nicholas carefully disengaged himself, and stood from the lounge – but when Dave went to get up, too, Nicholas said, "No, wait there."

Dave shivered in happy anticipation.

Nicholas returned in a few moments with a small bundle of things wrapped up in one of their silk slips, which he put down on the lounge out of Dave's reach before turning to stand in the middle of the room. "Come here," he gently asked Dave – and Dave happily went.

Nicholas leant in to brush a kiss across Dave's mouth, and then took Dave's face in both hands and kissed him hungrily, his tongue pushing out to lick across Dave's lips and then press inside. Dave sucked on him, rubbing his own tongue up against Nicholas's in a tender caress. Being so used to each other as they were, they hardly needed anything more than that to get in the mood.

More kisses pressed to his face, and Nicholas's hands running lightly across his shoulders, down to his waist – and then grasping the hem of his t-shirt and slowly lifting it up and off. Nicholas dropped to his knees, and grinned happily up at Dave while unbuttoning and unzipping Dave's jeans – and then his jeans and boxers were carefully eased down past his hip bones, past his cock already heavy with interest, and slid down his thighs and further until at last he could step out of them and stand there naked.

Nicholas stood, still dressed in jeans and t-shirt. "Your turn?" Dave asked, lifting his hands.

"Not yet," Nicholas replied with a smile that hinted at very thorough plans. He went over to the things he'd put on the lounge, and came back with the silk stockings. "All right?"

"I said anything," Dave replied – though he'd only worn these once before, and it had been on the strict understanding that Nicholas never asked Dave to shave his legs. 'As if,' Nicholas had scornfully retorted.

Nicholas knelt again, and gathered up one of the stockings, hands effortlessly rhythmic. Once he was ready, Dave lifted one foot, resting a hand on Nicholas's shoulder for balance, and watched as Nicholas carefully fitted the stocking over Dave's toes, settled it into place. Then he eased the sheer pale gold silk up Dave's leg, shaping it perfectly, until the top was snug around Dave's thigh. Nicholas reached for a ribbon, and tied it around the stocking to hold it in place with a golden bow. More kisses pressed to the bare skin above the silk, with an occasional 'accidental' nudge of nose or cheek against Dave's cock which hung thickly over his balls. Then the other leg received the same attentions, before Nicholas stood. A third ribbon was tied around Dave's left arm, about as high as it would go, and Nicholas caught up the long loose lengths in bow after bow.

Then, taking each of Dave's hands in his and holding them a little way out to each side as if to put Dave on display, Nicholas smiled at him with an appreciative twinkle in his eyes. "You really are the most gorgeous creature ..."

"Not better than butterflies," Dave protested, his voice already a bit rough.

"Better than butterflies," Nicholas confirmed with a nod.

To which Dave had no sensible response. But that was all right, because after a moment Nicholas pressed a kiss to his mouth, and then headed back to the lounge.

He returned with the butt plug and lube. "All right?" he asked again.

Dave simply nodded, and Nicholas walked around to kneel behind him, to kiss him *there* – and then, with the confidence of long familiarity, Nicholas broached him with two lubed fingers and then eased the plug inside. It sat snug within, filling him and promising there was more to come. Dave shivered a little – and Nicholas, who still knelt behind him, tapped his fingers against the plug's base, which turned the shiver into a shudder. Dave let out a sharp breath –

"No, come on," Nicholas murmured, pressing a kiss to Dave's rear. "Tonight I want to hear you."

Well, he'd feel foolish if he tried to manufacture a groan now, so Dave promised, "Next time."

"Good." Nicholas pressed another kiss to his skin – and then took a bite of flesh, not hard but startling.

"Ow!" cried Dave.

"Good," Nicholas repeated complacently. "That's more like it." Then he stood, and came around to smile with happy mischief at Dave, to take his hand. "Let's go to bed."

Dave happily followed him down the hall, walking only a little bit gingerly …

Nicholas had Dave lie down in the middle of the bed, and then knelt beside him to use silk cords to tie each of Dave's wrists to the wooden slats of the bedhead directly above him. Dave tugged on the cords carefully as Nicholas drew away again, testing their firmness. They held – though as with the ribbons, they were only fastened with bows, and Dave could undo them himself at any time, if he needed to.

Nicholas pulled away again and stood, watching Dave with a bright heavy gaze as he took off his own clothes – and a moment later Nicholas was on all fours on the bed beside him, stealing a kiss from his mouth, then pushing down further to nuzzle at Dave's throat … Dave stretched tall in anticipation, luxuriating in the flex of his lower spine, feeling the weight and slight pressure of the plug within him – and he moaned a little encouragement as Nicholas unerringly found that particular place at the juncture of his neck and shoulder … moaned under his breath – until Nicholas took another bite at him, which provoked a grunt of protest, and then a muttered, "All right, all right!"

A rumbling kind of purr answered him, and then with slow deliberation Nicholas worked his way further down Dave's body, kissing and licking and nibbling at all the places he knew would drive Dave mad with wanting. It was enough incitement to have Dave making a needy little noise on each panting breath. By the time Nicholas was lapping at Dave's tackle, his cock was hot and hard and so damned *ready* … Nicholas was still taking his time, though, and would not be hurried along even though Dave wriggled impatiently, and rolled his hips, and pushed up against where Nicholas's hands were pinning him down.

At last Nicholas deigned to take Dave's cockhead into his mouth, and suckle it sweetly – but only for a few moments. Dave growled, and tugged at the restraints that meant he couldn't clutch at Nicholas or drag him closer.

"You've been doing very nicely," Nicholas commented, looking up at him from beyond Dave's proudly-standing cock. "Still a bit quiet, mind you – but I'm sure I'll have you shouting before long."

"Nnn," Dave said, in some disgruntlement.

"Words," Nicholas continued. "I think for now we need words."

Dave frowned at him suspiciously. "What words?"

"How about … you tell me what you want … and I'll do it."

A silence dragged – in which Nicholas did nothing but continue looking with confident hope up at Dave.

"And, you know …" Nicholas helpfully continued, "I won't do anything unless you tell me."

Dave shook his head. "Can't."

"No?"

"No! We won't end up doing *anything*!"

"Now, come on. You're not the shy inarticulate Aussie bloke you sometimes pretend to be. At least, not with *me*."

"I can't, Nicholas," Dave insisted. And to underscore his point, he glanced at his own cock, which had wilted a little. "I don't have the words. Not for this kind of thing."

"Well, then," Nicholas replied. "Never mind all that." And he obligingly bent his head to encourage Dave back into full-blooded life, with a hand slipping in below to roll and tug at his balls in a rhythm that had a fingertip regularly nudging at the base of the plug, sending a delicious vibration deep within him – and Dave played his part, at first embarrassed to be making an effort to translate sensations into sounds … but it felt surprisingly good, and the sounds transformed back into new sensations, quite apart from Nicholas rewarding him with exactly the right steady increase in intensity, and his free hand sliding up Dave's chest to pinch and rub at a nipple.

"Soon," Dave was eventually saying – though Nicholas seemed to only take this as a prompt to slow down. "Please," Dave was begging.

"*Mmm …*" Nicholas happily murmured around Dave's cock.

And still it went on and on, these thunderously awesome pleasures, until Dave began to fear that the final lightning strike would never quite happen. "*Please*, Nicholas …"

"*Mmm … !*"

And maybe Nicholas did want the words after all – "Please," Dave muttered – so then he gathered himself up tight and blurted, "Seize the fucking day, Nicholas – *right fucking now.*"

Which had exactly the opposite effect Dave had intended. Nicholas's mouth slid up off Dave's cock leaving it standing there damp with saliva and feeling the cold even on this warm day – and Nicholas sat up a little, while his hands kept working away at what they'd been doing, though gently now. "*Some* things," said Nicholas, with a smile that was probably a little shakier than Nicholas would have wanted, "are worth taking one's time over."

Dave really was out of words, so he just gazed up at Nicholas mutely, probably looking completely pitiful, for Nicholas kind of chuckled half-heartedly and then carefully withdrew his hands. At Dave's bereft protest, which sounded disconcertingly like a whimper, Nicholas nodded reassuringly – and he reached for the lube, and reached down between his own thighs to prepare himself.

"Soon," Nicholas whispered. "Soon, I promise."

And already he was straddling Dave's hips, and positioning himself – they didn't do this often, but it was often enough for it to all be quite instinctive – and then pushing down and further down onto Dave, taking him in and deeper in. Dave was all tensed up at this point, and virtually breathless with it, gazing up at his glorious contrary husband, and feeling the pressures of both having and being had … As soon as Nicholas was settled, he reached behind himself to play with Dave's balls, before at last beginning to rock his hips in a subtle move that threatened imminent devastation.

"Nicholas –" Dave said, his voice breaking with need and wonder.

"Ssh … it's all right."

Nicholas's cock bobbed stiffly as he moved, and Dave eyed it hungrily, wondering what Nicholas's plans were for his own pleasure. Perhaps he would toss himself off – but his right hand was currently toying with Dave's nipple again, and judging by the weight behind it, Dave thought Nicholas was pretty much propping himself upright at this point.

"Nicholas –" he tried again.

"Yes," Nicholas eventually said. After another moment or two, he managed to pause in his rhythm and lean forward far enough to pull at one of the cords, which fell free of the bedhead. Once Nicholas had resumed his chosen tasks, he nodded again at Dave, and said, "Make me come."

"My pleasure," Dave replied. And he reached down with the silk still binding his wrist, and bound his hand around Nicholas's gorgeous cock, and – after taking a moment to find the right timing – Dave began deliberately working away at a task that would be over all too soon.

Sure enough, Nicholas's head dropped back with a resounding groan, and his rhythms faltered – intensified for a moment – stilled – and then he was spurting his seed across Dave's belly, groaning again – and his tight arse was clutching at Dave's cock, Dave's own arse was clutching at the plug, Nicholas's hand was trembling on Dave's tender balls – and suddenly the end was upon him at last, and Dave drove up into Nicholas with a shout, and then another, all joy and relief and love …

They finally collapsed together – Nicholas barely summoning the energy to deal with the plug, but he did so while Dave released his other wrist – and Dave wrapped both arms around this awesome man, his husband, murmuring some nonsense about him being the best fuck in all the world, "the best lover ever", to which Nicholas murmured something that sounded pleased. And they settled there together in their bed, in their home, and after a while – forgetting all about that midnight snack – they slept.

The next morning saw Dave and Nicholas at the airport early to collect Robin. They joined the line-up leaning on the waist-high barriers, greeted with nods and friendly monosyllables from the drivers and tour operators and such, some of whom had known Dave since he was a kid. "Brought the missus with you, then?" one of them commented to Dave.

Nicholas snorted with quiet humour, but Dave answered seriously enough. "Yeah, his nephew's coming to visit for his summer holidays. Well, you know … it's winter here, summer up there."

"Got everything arse-about, them Poms."

"You just wait," Nicholas muttered darkly. "The magnetic poles will reverse, and then where will you be?"

"Still in God's own country, mate!"

"So you will," Nicholas happily responded. "And so will I!"

There was a general round of laughter, and then everyone fell back to their earlier silence or desultory talk. Nicholas nudged Dave with an elbow, and indicated the cold hard floor on the other side of the barriers. "That's where I was when I saw you for the very first time."

The guy on the other side of Dave asked, "Love at first sight, was it?"

"I get a lot of that," Dave remarked.

"What can you do?" was the sympathetic response.

"I fancied him so badly!" Nicholas declared. "It wasn't love, I don't suppose – not back then. But that's where it began. That's where our story began."

A resounding silence greeted this. *Far* too much information to be sharing with Aussie blokes of either gender. Dave was blushing, a little, but he couldn't deny that he was pleased. No doubt his own smile was as fond as one of Nicholas's, despite him trying to repress it. He hardly knew where to look.

But finally someone snorted, and someone else spluttered into laughter, and the embarrassment was lost in the general hubbub, or maybe just transformed into something else, something better. "Someone's overdone it with the coffee this morning," was one comment. – "That's why I never bring my missus along," another observed. – "Jeez, there's a decent hour and a private place for that kind of thing …"

Dave and Nicholas leant there on the barrier together, pressed shoulder to shoulder, letting the jibes wash over them. And eventually Dave dared to glance at his husband, and he saw Nicholas's lips curling in infinite amusement … and Dave could hardly even begin to measure his own happiness. He hadn't seen the edges of it for *years*.

"Nicholas!"

Finally Robin appeared, dressed in pale blue jeans, a pale pink polo shirt and a white jumper, pushing a trolley loaded with bags. A moment later Robin and Nicholas were dashing down either side of the barrier to at last meet in a massive hug, and Robin was babbling on at a million miles an hour, and only lifting his head from where it had been tucked against Nicholas's for the sake of gazing at his beloved uncle with tears in his eyes. He was as tall as Nicholas now, which was astonishing, though it seemed that his face hadn't kept pace with the rest of him, and Robin still looked rather younger than his years. It was kind of adorable to watch him drop a kiss on the tip of Nicholas's nose and then share a giggle.

"So," someone pondered, "are they *all* gay, then?" – "Couldn't be," someone else replied. "They'd have died out centuries ago."

Dave chuckled as he stood. "Just these two, in this family, I think."

"And yourself, mate."

"And myself," he agreed with a nod.

The first thing Robin did when they reached the car was to shuck off his jumper. "I thought it was meant to be winter here," he commented, lifting a quizzical hand to take in the warm bright sunny day.

"It *is* winter here," Dave confirmed.

Robin guffawed – and then he hardly quit talking the entire drive home, pausing only every now and then to allow Nicholas to get a response in or a question of his own. First the long flight and the stopover in Singapore were gone over in great detail. Nicholas interrupted at some point to ask, "Have you texted Simon to say you're here safely?"

"Oh, no. I'll do that now." And Robin proceeded to tap out a text on his smartphone while still talking away. He meandered his way into commentary on the family news, most of which Nicholas and Dave had already heard via one source or another.

Nicholas managed to restrain himself until they were turning in to their own road before asking, "And Frank? How's Frank doing?"

"Oh my God, he's a granddad now! Gemma had a baby girl."

"Yes, Simon emailed me. They're all well?"

"Absolutely. And Frank is like … *besotted*. I never got that before, about a parent or whatever falling in love with their child. Until I saw Frank, and it's like … his heart is no longer his own."

"I'm glad," Nicholas said, turning to look out the side window – but not before Dave glimpsed Nicholas's achingly poignant smile.

Robin quietened at last as Nicholas took him to the bedroom that would be his for the next three months – the one that used to be Dave's when he was growing up. Later on, while Dave's dad was still alive, Denise had moved in and shared the room with Dave, so it contained a double bed and wasn't filled with as much childish clutter as Robin might have expected.

Once Robin had shed his gear, Nicholas showed him around the rest of the house. "This is really nice!" was Robin's verdict as they joined Dave in the kitchen.

Dave handed him a cup of tea. "You sound surprised. Did you think I'd have Nicholas living in a corrugated iron shack?"

"No! No, of course not." Robin looked around him again, at the kitchen and family room, and the backyard full of greenery. "I've seen photos, of course, and everyone who's visited said it's great – but I didn't get to *feel* it until now. And it feels like home."

"It does, doesn't it?" Nicholas quietly agreed. "I felt that right away, too."

"Huh," said Dave, handing his husband a cup of coffee. "How I remember it is, the first time I brought you here, you promptly changed your plane tickets and went back to England six weeks early."

Nicholas took the coffee, put it down, and grabbed Dave's hand. "I *wanted* to stay – forever."

Dave coloured a little under Nicholas's earnest gaze – all too aware of

Robin's wistful yearning. "And now you can," Dave replied a little too brusquely. "Now you are." Then he cleared his throat and changed the subject. "Are you hungry, Robin? I thought I'd cook us a proper breakfast this morning. Eggs, bacon, sausages, toast …"

Robin brightened immediately. "Marmalade and extra toast for after … ?"

"And marmalade for after," Dave confirmed.

"See?" Nicholas commented to Robin. "He makes all our wishes come true."

The perils of having a house guest were soon made evident. Dave had done a load of washing on the morning of that first day, and had hung the bulk of it on the Hills Hoist in the backyard. A few items, however, the hand-washed silk items, he hung on the clothes airer and tucked it away out of sight in the main bedroom. He left the door open, as usual during the day, but assumed Robin would know better than to walk in uninvited …

Dave discovered he'd been wrong about that when Robin wandered into the family room with the toe of one of the silk stockings pinched between thumb and forefinger and held at arm's length, his expression squeamish. Dave abruptly turned waratah red, and sat down on the nearest available chair.

"Unc-le Nich-o-laaas …" Robin drawled.

Nicholas looked up from the newspaper he'd been reading, and promptly turned coldly unimpressed.

"You don't really *wear* these, do you?" Robin sounded more creeped out than disgusted, but still. It wasn't pleasant. "I never knew you were into *drag* …"

"*Not* that it's any of your business," Nicholas tartly replied, turning a page of the newspaper, "but so what if I do?"

"Seriously? I always thought you were … a man. A man who liked men."

"Things are generally a little more complicated than that," Nicholas replied in somewhat softer tones. He'd had the mercy to not even glance at Dave through all this. "I think you'll find … there are infinite varieties of men and women and those in between."

"But *you're* not complicated," Robin insisted, letting his hand drop now.

"You've always been completely straightforward! Completely honest!"

"My darling, I'd rather be complicated than narrow-minded. Now, you go and put that back where you found it – *respectfully*, thank you – and then you can have a bit of a think about your reactions. I would have expected rather more acceptance, coming from *you*."

There was a brief struggling silence, and then at last Robin said in a humbled voice, "Yes, Uncle Nicholas. Sorry." And he turned and headed back down the hallway. A couple of moments later, the door to the guest bedroom could be heard to firmly close in what was, in context, a chagrined slam.

Nicholas continued reading the newspaper, letting Dave process all of that in whatever ways he needed to.

Eventually, after Nicholas turned another page, Dave asked quietly, "D'you mind him thinking that? I mean, that you're the one who wears them?"

Nicholas looked up at Dave, his gaze direct and relaxed, his smile gentle. "No, I don't mind. Don't worry about it."

Dave had to admire the man's insouciance. He shuddered in a belated reaction, and went to put the kettle on. And then he said, "You know, we still all have a lot to learn from you."

Nicholas shone a crinkly smile in his direction that did away with the last of Dave's anxieties.

two

Two days later Dave drove the Toyota Land Cruiser down the Warrego Highway, with Nicholas beside him in the passenger seat – and Robin in the back, paying far more attention to his smartphone than to the passing countryside. Nicholas caught Dave's glance, and twisted around for a moment to watch Robin sitting there with his head down … Dave wondered if Nicholas was remembering, as Dave himself was, so very strongly, the first time he'd driven Nicholas down this road. *That* visiting Englishman had stared out the window, not wanting to miss a single detail of the scenery. *This* one seemed more concerned about not missing his friends' updated Facebook statuses.

Nicholas snorted. "Well – if you must – enjoy it while you can," he advised. "There's coverage in Charleville, but once we get near the waterhole, you won't get any signal at all."

Robin looked up at him with a woebegone face. "Not even a single bar?"

"No."

"Oh my God! *How* long are we staying there … ?"

"Five or six days, I think." Nicholas glanced at Dave to confirm this.

"We're leaving a day earlier than I'd planned," said Dave, "so we can spend six at the waterhole – as long as Charlie's okay with that."

"*God* …" Robin grumbled.

Nicholas turned around in his seat so he was facing the front again. "This is a privilege, you know. I hope you appreciate it! David hasn't taken anyone but me and Charlie to the waterhole in all these years."

"Oh." That had caught Robin's attention. "Why not?" he asked Dave.

Oddly enough, Dave found that he didn't have a ready answer. A beat of silence passed.

"It's a very special place," Nicholas supplied. "You've heard David and Charlie talk about the Dreaming … ? The waterhole is a sacred site."

"So, like … Aboriginal people go there?"

Another beat of silence.

"Well," said Nicholas. "It's quite difficult to find. Only David really knows the way."

"Not even you, Nicholas?"

"I don't drive, remember? Well, David taught me, but only for emergencies. And it's too far from anywhere to walk there. I've never even tried to get there on my own. I've never had to!"

"Oh." And Robin gazed out the side window rather pensively, his phone lying forgotten in his cupped hands.

If Dave had thought Robin looked afraid of being so far distant from civilisation, he would have offered reassurance. As it was, he let the peaceful silence grow. Nicholas quietly reached to rest a hand on Dave's thigh … and they drove on into the Outback.

They took their time with the journey, and reached Charleville on the second day. Once they'd checked in with Marge at the hotel, Robin started bouncing around insisting they go meet Charlie – "*Now*. Right now. Come *on*, guys."

Nicholas exchanged an indulgent smile-and-shrug with Dave, and obviously they had no objections to the plan, so they all headed down to the pub.

Charlie was sitting at their usual table, as if he'd known when they'd show up. He stood to greet them, and returned Robin's enthusiastic hug in kind. "Look at you!" he marvelled once they'd parted, looking over Robin from top to toe. "You're a man now."

Robin snorted. "I was, like, *eleven* last time we met!"

"So you were …" Charlie equably agreed.

"Charlie, I'll get us a beer," said Dave. "Nicholas?"

"Yes, please," said Nicholas, with a smile happily anticipating a treat. He didn't drink very often at all, but Dave knew well enough there was something about being in the Outback that called for a cool pour of amber.

"Robin? What d'you want to drink?"

"I'll have a beer, too, please. May I?"

Dave nodded, though he asked, "Have you got ID?"

"I have my driving licence. English, though."

"That's fine. Come to the bar with me, all right? Rosie will want to check it."

They drew a few stares, of course. Dave still attracted a bit of benign bemusement, and had done ever since he'd taken up with Nicholas; he'd long been used to letting that be. Robin, though, was a new face to ponder, and almost everything about him declared he was a visitor – not least the fact that he refused to wear his new Akubra indoors. This was despite Robin thinking he looked pretty cool in it, with which Dave had to agree. The young fella had insisted on the Graphite Grey, which Dave felt was too dark for practical purposes – but then Robin lived in England, so it wasn't as if he needed it all year round.

"You right, Dave?" asked Rosie when she reached them.

"Yeah, thanks. This is Robin." He nudged Robin with an elbow, prompting him to hand over his ID. "He's legal."

Rosie considered the card for a long moment, and then lifted her chin in acknowledgement as she handed it back. "What'll it be, Dave?"

"Four Cascades, thanks, mate."

The bloke sitting near them on a barstool had been gazing sideways at Dave this whole time. Dave offered him a brief nod, wondering if the guy was simply curious about the ocker who'd married the son of an English earl. Maybe that wasn't it, though, as eventually the guy asked, "New client, Mr Taylor?"

Dave's brow rose in surprise, as he was pretty sure they'd never met before – but he readily answered, "No, Robin's family. Not a business trip, this time."

Rosie came back with the beers, so Dave left it at that. He paid, exchanged polite nods all round, then he and Robin took the beers back to their table and settled in.

After they'd all taken their first appreciative mouthful, Charlie asked Robin, "You're here for the winter?"

"Yes, it's our summer holidays back home. The 'long vacation'. Dad said he'd pay for me to come here, if I got three A levels at grade A. And I did." Robin added with cheeky pride, "Actually, I got four!"

"Good for you," said Charlie, apparently understanding more about what that meant than Dave did.

"I had, like, a conditional offer from Oxford, so of course I was always gonna totally blitz it … Dad didn't need to bribe me," he added with a beaming grin, "but I wasn't complaining!"

"It wasn't bribery," Nicholas said, correcting him. "It was a reward."

"Whatever. It meant I got to come see you – at *last* …"

The two of them looked fondly at each other, and Nicholas said something soft that was meant for Robin alone.

Dave was feeling just as fond, but he took the opportunity to turn to Charlie and quietly ask, "That guy at the bar next to where I was standing … You know him?"

Charlie took another mouthful of beer, and discreetly lifted his gaze as he did so. "Yeah – know of him, anyway. Ted Walinski. Works as a surveyor."

"Huh," said Dave. "Never even heard of him."

"Why d'you ask?"

"He knows me! Well, my name, anyway, and what I do." Dave shrugged. "I don't suppose it matters, but if I meet someone through the business, I try to remember them, you know?"

"That's the smart thing to do," Charlie agreed, before they turned to more interesting concerns.

The next morning saw Dave driving down towards Cunnamulla, with Nicholas beside him and Charlie and Robin in the back. Nicholas's smile had a happy anticipatory kick to it, as it always did when they were heading for the waterhole. Charlie's usual cheerfulness was in full bubble, and even Robin had put his phone away to engage with the countryside and his companions.

"So, what's this place called?" Robin asked at some point about an hour into the journey.

Charlie replied, "It doesn't have a white-fella name."

"What's its black-fella name, then?" Robin persisted.

Dave glanced at Charlie via the rear-view mirror, but Charlie was the last person to take unnecessary offence when someone was genuinely interested and willing to learn. Nevertheless, Dave said, "We call the Indigenous people around here 'Murri', Robin, yeah?"

"Oh. Yeah, okay. What's its Murri name, Charlie?"

Charlie grinned at him. "Only your Uncle Davey and me know that."

"What, not even Nicholas?"

"Not even Nicholas," Charlie confirmed. He seemed to ponder this for a moment, and Dave himself was prompted to wonder whether or when that should change. They'd kind of coasted along together on the current arrangements for a few years now – but who would he and Charlie pass the Dreamtime knowledge to, when it was time?

"What about –" Robin continued. "I mean, isn't there a tribe that belongs there?"

"Nah, there was but they're lost to us, mate. I had a friend, he was the last of 'em. He's the one who passed the songs to me. And I passed them on to Davey, because he was the one who found the place, when I never could."

"Wow," said Robin, gazing at Dave with a new level of respect.

Dave turned his head for a moment to acknowledge Robin with a rueful nod – and he caught Nicholas's proudly glowing grin in the corner of his eye on the way back. Dave had been staggered and humbled when Charlie first suggested all of this, and Dave remained so now. He caught up Nicholas's hand from where it rested on his thigh, and without taking his eyes from the road lifted it to his lips for a kiss. Nicholas returned the favour, bringing their joined hands over to his own mouth to press a kiss to the back of Dave's hand, before returning it to the wheel and his hand to Dave's thigh.

"Okay," Robin continued once they were done. "So we're gonna be holding our own … like, mini corroboree or something?"

"Well," said Dave. "Charlie and I are."

"But I can watch, right?"

"I'm afraid not, Robin."

Charlie offered, "Some of it, he could, Davey."

Robin was unimpressed. "I bet you let Nicholas watch!"

"Huh," Dave huffed. "Yeah, but I shouldn't. Strictly speaking. So, don't tell Charlie, okay?"

Charlie just guffawed, as if he'd known it all along.

Nicholas diplomatically said, "You and I, Robin, we'll do the right thing and sit this one out."

Silence.

"It's *important*, Robin," Nicholas continued. "It's not just for fun."

"Yeah riiight …" Robin drawled, turning away to stare out the window.

They just let him be after that. But from what Dave could see, Robin was doing more pondering than sulking. So maybe that was all right.

They stopped for lunch in Cunnamulla, indulging in cheesecake afterwards for no better reason than that they wouldn't be eating such things for a while. Then Dave filled up the Cruiser with petrol, and they headed west.

About half an hour out of town, Dave saw a sand-coloured Land Rover Discovery parked on the other side of the road, facing towards them. He slowed down a bit to see if anyone was in trouble. Nothing seemed wrong with the vehicle at least. However, the driver wasn't in sight.

"Call of nature?" Charlie surmised.

"Doesn't look like a flat tyre, anyway," Dave said.

"Careful …" Charlie murmured when Dave slowed down further.

"Yeah," he replied shortly. "Nicholas. Can you see anything on your side? Scan, like, the full one-eighty. Robin, you have a look, too."

"All right." Nicholas sounded a bit puzzled, but he obligingly shifted in his seat, and the two Englishmen looked around. "I can't see anything but scrub and dirt. Robin?"

"Nothing, Uncle David."

"What are we looking for, exactly?"

But then just as they drew near the Land Rover, a figure stepped around from the far side of it, with a thermos and cup in his hands. It was the surveyor who'd spoken to Dave in the pub.

Dave let out a pent-up breath, and pulled to a stop, powering down his window to talk to the man. "You all right? Walinski, isn't it?"

"That's right, Mr Taylor." The man lifted one hand to push his hat back on his head, the better to hold a conversation. "Ted Walinski." He fixed the cup back on the thermos, and then reached to shake Dave's hand before offering a general nod to the others.

"You're all right out here? Not broken down, or anything?"

"No, she's right. Just felt like a cuppa, and didn't want to wait for Cunnamulla. Thanks for checking, though."

"No worries." Dave nodded, and after a beat of silence that wasn't filled, he said, "See ya round, then."

"Yeah. Thanks again!" Walinski stepped back, and lifted his hand in farewell.

Dave pulled away, and quickly eased up to his regular speed. He kept half an eye on the rear-view mirror, though, and noticed that Charlie had turned to watch as much as he could through his side window. Not that Walinski was doing anything more than pouring himself another cup of tea.

"All right?" Dave said to Charlie as the Land Rover receded to little more than a dot.

"Yeah," Charlie replied, resettling himself.

Nicholas was watching Dave with wary curiosity, but obviously knew better than to ask with Robin in hearing distance. And Dave wasn't even sure how much he wanted to tell Nicholas about ambushes and kidnappings and other nefarious things.

After another moment, Charlie turned to Robin. "D'you want me to teach you one of the songs your Uncle David's gonna be singing at the waterhole?"

"Hell, yes!" was the delighted reply.

Although some of the approach to the waterhole still felt counter-intuitive, Dave pretty much had the hang of it by now. There was a place where he always felt he had to turn right but knew he had to turn left, and another place where his instincts were to turn left which was actually correct. There was a worn old ridge of rocks like a skeletal spine poking out of the ground that he had to follow – it even had a kind of arrowhead formation at the far end – and he'd have to ask Charlie about all of that, because if he had the meaning right, the formation might actually feature in one of the songs. Then he had to pay careful attention to feel the gentle rise of the ground and drive at the correct angle up across it – and there would be nothing for a while, absolutely nothing. But then, finally, just as he was beginning to really give in to the doubt, the Land Cruiser would crest the edge of the wide flat valley that cradled their waterhole, and he would marvel at the fact that he'd managed the impossible yet again.

Nicholas and Charlie each let out a long sigh of relief as if they'd hardly even dared breathe for the past five minutes. Dave chuckled, and they did, too – and Robin was looking around him in vain for a miraculous change in the landscape, and asking, "What? What happened? Where are we?"

"We're almost at the waterhole," Dave said, shifting down a gear and then easing the Cruiser across onto the long shallow slope.

"It's right ahead of us," Nicholas added, pointing. "See the denser foliage there? That's the treetops breaking above ground level."

"No …" Robin answered uncertainly, leaning forward as far as he could to align his sight down Nicholas's arm.

"Never mind. We'll be there in a few minutes. Just keep watching."

"What I reckon," Dave said conversationally – "not that I did anything more than high school geography. What I reckon is that a meteor hit, thousands or ten-thousands –" He looked doubtingly at Nicholas.

"Tens of thousands," Nicholas supplied.

"Yeah, that many years ago. And the meteor created this whole big crater – though it's been so long that it's fairly worn down now. And the meteor made the original hole there, too, and maybe it became a sinkhole, or opened up a cave system or something. And the depth of it means it's right near the underground water table, and *that's* what feeds the actual waterhole."

"Yeah … ?" said Robin, apparently taking all of that in.

"Did you do geology?" Dave asked him.

"Yeah, a bit. I get what you're saying."

"Cos there's very little rain out here, hardly any run-off. But the actual waterhole itself is always full. It's always at the same level. So I reckon the water table somehow replenishes it."

"That's awesome," said Robin.

Dave laughed. "It is pretty awesome," he agreed. They were almost there now. He turned to the left once he could see the cliff edge, found the track that led down into the waterhole, but then pulled the Cruiser up and parked it nearby. He looked around at his companions. "It's Robin's first time here. What d'you say we walk down there, so he gets the full impact?"

"Absolutely," Nicholas said, his eyes as bright as his beautiful smile. He was already opening the door and swinging those long legs out and grabbing up his Akubra, all in one smooth move. The others followed suit, and a moment later the four of them were crossing over a slight ridge and then following the worn old layer of rock that served as a track down into the waterhole.

They walked in silence for a while, feeling the slightly cooler temperature as soon as they were below ground level and out of the direct sun. The cliff wall climbed steeply above them, a rich reddish-black, the edge of it sharp against the bright blue sky. Soon they reached the twist in the track that took them back around to the right.

Nicholas was grinning in anticipation, though even Dave knew it was the wrong season to be expecting to find anything more than the hibernating pupae of his butterflies. "Isn't this marvellous?" Nicholas asked Robin in hushed tones.

Charlie chuckled under his breath –

But Robin shivered. "It's kind of … well, not creepy, I guess."

"There's a magic here," Nicholas said.

"Okay, it's creepy," Robin concluded.

"It's not … familiar," Nicholas offered. "But you'll get used to it. Anyway. David belongs here, and so does Charlie, and they're happy that we're here, so the waterhole will be, too."

Robin was looking somewhat sceptical.

Charlie tilted his head as if considering or listening, and then announced, "Old man grunter, he's happy that you're here. This is his place, see?"

With more politeness than belief, Robin asked, "He's the Ancestor, right?"

"Right. He's sleeping down deep in the waterhole, he's a long time dreaming …"

Which, despite his obvious efforts to restrain himself, made Robin shiver all over again.

Dave tried another tack. "Well, how much d'you remember of your geology, Robin?"

"A bit."

"See the colours of the cliff walls and the rocks? What kind of stone d'you think that is?"

Robin scrunched up his face for a moment as he looked around. "Iron ore … ?"

"Exactly!"

"Which goes to make steel, doesn't it?"

"Yes! Well. I don't know for sure that it's iron ore, but that's my guess." They were walking through the trees and ground cover now, and then at last they were out in the open and approaching the jewel-bright pool of water itself. "I think the meteor – if that's what happened – drilled down into here."

Robin gasped. "You mean, it might still be down there, at the bottom of the pond? The meteor itself?"

"Maybe."

"Well, haven't you swum down there, to try to find it?"

The three adults were all completely taken aback by the notion.

"No," said Nicholas. "We don't disturb anything we don't have to."

"But –" said Robin.

"The Ancestor is dreaming down there," said Charlie. "It's not for us to wake him."

"But –"

"Anyway, the water's not safe," Dave concluded rather flatly. "Don't drink it, all right? We hardly even take a dip when we're here."

Robin sighed, and scuffed one sneakered foot through the dirt. "All right, all right," he mumbled.

A moment's silence fell heavily through them.

But then Nicholas said, with barely controlled excitement, "Shall I show you the butterflies? They're in their pupal stage at the moment."

Robin smiled at him indulgently, and peace returned. "Yes, please, Uncle Nicholas." And Dave watched as Robin slipped his hand into Nicholas's and the two of them headed further past the pool, past the old rockfall, and on towards the wattle.

When Dave announced he was going to head up and fetch the Cruiser, Robin got all panicky again. "You're not bringing it down here?!"

"Yeah, I am."

"But – how?"

"Down the same track we just walked."

Robin cast a wide-eyed stare at what little they could see of the old layer of rock through the foliage, and especially at where the track turned a corner near the bottom.

Dave scoffed a gentle laugh. "It's no worse than those narrow twisty lanes you call roads in England. In fact, it's better, cos at least you're not running along blindly between two great hedgerows."

"But – what if something goes wrong? Like another landslide," he added, gesturing behind him at the long-ago tumble of rocks. "How will we get out?"

"Robin," Dave said, "nothing's changed in here in the last seven years. Nothing but the trees slowly growing, and the butterflies emerging twice a year. I can't remember seeing even one fresh rock added to that fall over there."

"Yeah?"

"In fact, *that's* what used to not sit right with me. How everything stays the same. There aren't even any animals around to disturb things …" An edgy silence made Dave realise he'd better shut up sooner rather than later. "But that's good, right?" he tried. "What you see is what you get, no more and no less."

"Huh," said Robin.

"Well, anyway," Dave blundered on, given that neither Nicholas nor Charlie were gonna help him out, "if we're not back in Brisbane in a few days, Denise will call out the troops."

Robin squinted at him suspiciously. "I thought you were the only person who can find this place."

Dave assumed a lofty pose and told a white lie. "I left her detailed instructions, just in case."

At which Charlie snorted a chuckle, and Nicholas shook his head, ducking to hide a wry smile – so Robin was convinced. In fact, with what had to be youthful enthusiasm, he seemed to have a complete change of heart. "So, can I come with you, then? I wanna see how you get round that turn!"

Dave snorted, too. "Sure. Come on, then." And he escorted Robin back up the track, with the young fella chattering on as if he didn't have a care in the world.

They set up their campsite, Dave and Nicholas working with an efficiency based on years of shared habits, and Robin helping where he could. Nicholas helped Robin set up his own tent, which made Dave smile, remembering the first time Nicholas had helped Dave set up an earlier example of the same model. That was when Dave had first realised that Nicholas was stronger than he appeared; yet another small step on the long road to falling in love, had he but known it at the time.

Soon Nicholas and Robin had set up a second tent nearby. "So, this is for you two?" Robin asked.

"Well, no," Nicholas replied. "Dave and I like to sleep on a mattress on top of the Cruiser."

Robin's mouth twisted in distaste as he picked up on Nicholas's hint of self-consciousness. "What, out in the open? Where either of us could see you two … getting it on?"

"Don't worry. I should think we can manage to restrain ourselves for a few days."

"You'd better!" Robin insisted. "I'm not hiding in my tent the whole time, and I didn't sign up for the full scenic tour!"

Nicholas manfully tried not to laugh, but then he glimpsed Dave's amusement and ended up spluttering in mirth. "I can assure you, Robin, that our tour guide comes highly recommended!"

"Uncle Nicholas …" Robin said forebodingly.

"No, you're right. We'll promise to behave."

Robin shrugged his acquiescence. Then, after a moment, he indicated the second tent. "What's this for, then? In case it rains?"

"It probably won't rain. This is Charlie's tent."

Robin turned to find Charlie, where he was building a campfire for that evening. "You're sleeping *inside*?" He sounded scandalised.

"Yeah, and on that camp bed, too," Charlie replied, gesturing at where the bed waited to be unpacked and set up. "What, you think us black fellas all just lie down in the dirt to sleep?"

"Oh. No." Robin had gone red with shame. "Sorry."

"Ah, I'm messin' with ya," Charlie said with a chuckle, coming over to nudge warily at the bed with a toe. "Let's see if we can figure out how to put this together, eh? So my poor old bones can rest comfy tonight."

Robin offered him a tentative grin, which became a real one in response to Charlie's smile, and the two of them got to work.

On the day that Dave and Charlie would perform the Dreaming songs, Dave drove the Cruiser up out of the waterhole so that Nicholas and Robin could use it as their base. Robin slowly followed them on foot, exaggerating his reluctance for tragic effect.

Dave laughed under his breath, watching him, and turned to say quietly to Nicholas, "If he's going to be difficult, why don't you drive him out to where you can get a signal on his phone? That should cheer him up, to check in with his mates."

Nicholas looked a bit panicked. "*Me* drive him?"

"You know you can."

"You'd trust me with the Cruiser? What if I – ?"

"Of course I trust you with the Cruiser. You'll be fine. Remember what I said after our last driving lesson?"

"You'd trust me with your life."

"Exactly." That's what it had been about, after all. Dave liked to have backup plans for his backup plans, and he couldn't bear the thought of Nicholas stuck out there miles from anywhere if anything happened to Dave.

"But I've never – not without you in the passenger seat."

"You don't have to if you don't want to," Dave equably assured him. "It was just an idea. But I reckon you'd be fine. And won't Frank be proud to hear about it, from you or Robin?"

The corner of Nicholas's mouth betrayed him by twitching into a smile. "You know just where all my buttons are, don't you, David?"

"And exactly how to push them!" Dave grinned. "I figured that's why you married me."

They were alerted to Robin's presence by a groan. "Oh my God, don't you two ever give it a rest?"

"No, we don't," Nicholas tartly responded. "But don't worry. You can return the favour by being just as insufferable when you find your … special someone."

"Yeah right," Robin said with a scowl, before climbing into the back seat of the Cruiser with an enormous sigh.

Dave and Nicholas exchanged rueful looks, and Dave muttered, "We're not having any of our own, are we?"

Nicholas chuckled. "Don't worry. Only the sort we can give back."

"Have fun, then!" Dave said in brighter tones that would carry. "I'll come back up when we're done. We'll only be an hour or so."

"It's cool. We'll be fine. Enjoy yourself." And Nicholas kissed him, before heading over to the Cruiser.

When Dave turned for a last glimpse of him before descending into the waterhole, he was pleased to see Nicholas in the driver's seat, his hands and his gaze reacquainting themselves with the controls.

Dave knew the songs and dances by heart now. Within moments he had settled into a comfortable rhythm in tandem with Charlie, as they progressed down towards the pool, and then sang the story of the Ancestor that slept there.

Most of the Ancestors had emerged in human form during the Dreamtime, and the Barcoo grunter was no different. He had been woken to life when another Ancestor fell from the sky – Dave still wasn't too sure whether she was supposed to be a star or a bird or some other living creature, but obviously his pedantic white-fella mind linked her with the meteor which he thought had created the waterhole. The two Ancestors had loved each other and loved the land, wandering the area and singing the trees and shrubs into being. They bathed in the pool and mucked about together, splashing the water around so that the run-off formed the old creek beds that Dave could still trace today. Theirs was a barren love, until at last the fallen Ancestor had to return to her home in the sky. Old man grunter transformed into a fish, so that if he must be alone then he would sleep in the pool forever and remember the joy he'd felt there. But before he sank he cried a lament for his lost love, and his tears became the blue butterflies that still lived there even now.

That was Dave's favourite song: the lament and the beautiful things it created. It wrung his heart. Not that he ever told Charlie that, but no doubt Charlie could hear it in his voice.

There were another couple of songs that led them away from the waterhole again, and then they were done.

Dave had been conscious in the midst of the songs of a head cautiously peeking over the cliff edge high above and peering down at them. He thought it was Robin; a short while later he was proved correct when Nicholas appeared beside him. Nicholas indulged himself by watching for a moment or two – with infinite fondness and respect – but then he turned away and took Robin with him. Dave continued on, undisturbed, and if Charlie had noticed he pretended not to.

Dave always felt a sense of peace after performing the songs and dances. There was a sense of satisfaction, even a feeling of reverence. He couldn't explain it to himself, because he knew well enough that he didn't believe in the literal truth of the Dreaming. Imagining himself as a small part of the ongoing story told by Aboriginal culture, however, was a gift and a comfort.

Charlie was quiet for a while after they'd finished as well. Dave had developed a habit of leaving him and wandering off to kneel by a particular rock near the waterhole. When the first of the blue butterflies they'd discovered had died, Dave had buried it under this flat stone. He'd never confessed as much to Nicholas, let alone to Charlie, but he'd never forgotten either.

Once he'd paid his respects, Dave wandered back to sit cross-legged by Charlie, and then when he thought the time was right, Dave finally broke the silence. "The first few songs … they're about finding the waterhole, aren't they?"

"Yeah." Charlie pondered on this for a short while. "That's what you call the songlines … The paths from one sacred site to another."

"Yeah."

"Didn't help me, though. When I was looking for the place before you found it? Couldn't make head nor tail of it."

"I was thinking that – there's a ridge of rocks sticking out of the dirt that we drive beside, that pretty much points the way here. And there's the song about the lizard that goes to sleep and is buried, only there's a curve of its body still above ground. So, are those two things related? Like, are the rocks what remain of the lizard … ?"

Charlie was grinning at him fondly, proudly, which was answer enough, and then he muttered once more, "Old man grunter chose well when he chose you, Davey."

While he couldn't really believe that, Dave appreciated the thought more than he could say, so he nodded in acceptance. "I'll show you the place when we're driving out."

When he climbed up out of the waterhole, it was to discover that Nicholas had been brave enough to drive the Cruiser out to the edge of the shallow crater after all. Dave watched as they slowly returned, Nicholas carefully finding a way through the scrub and between the rocks; being far more careful with the Cruiser's paintwork than even Dave ever was. Soon Dave could make out the frown of concentration on Nicholas's face – which turned into a full-beam smile as Nicholas finally pulled up near Dave.

"Told you you're wonderful," Dave said, reaching through the open window to give Nicholas's shoulder a gentle shake.

"I suppose that every now and then I can … *rise* to the occasion."

Robin groaned from the back seat. "Oh my God, save me."

Dave ignored him, and asked Nicholas, "Are you gonna drive her down into the waterhole, then?"

"Oh hell no," Nicholas brightly replied. And he clambered over onto the passenger seat, while Dave laughed and climbed up inside.

They left the waterhole a few days later – and they saw the Land Rover Discovery again, soon after they found their way back onto a sealed road. It was parked as before, although this time Ted Walinski was sitting perched on the bull bar, again with his thermos. He lifted a hand in casual greeting as they neared.

Dave slowed to a stop and lowered the window. "You right, mate?"

"Yeah, sure. You always catch me on a tea break."

"All right, then." Dave nodded a farewell. "See ya round."

"Thanks for stopping." Walinski offered them all a smile as Dave pulled the Cruiser away. "See ya!"

"What's he doing?" Dave asked Charlie a few moments later, as Charlie had turned to keep an eye on him.

Charlie said, "Maybe he's looking for our dust trail … He's not watching us, that's for sure."

Robin was all agog. "Could he, like, follow our tyre tracks back to the waterhole?"

"Maybe …" Charlie said.

"If he can find where I turned onto the road, then good luck to him. It was too stony to have left an impression."

"I know fellas who could find it."

"Yeah, and I know *you* could," Dave fondly agreed.

"David," said Nicholas in worried tones, "do you really think he could find his way there?"

"Well, honestly, if he does then he's accomplished something a lot of people have failed at."

"David –"

"It's not like we own the place," Dave argued. "And I can pretty much guarantee your butterflies will be safe. Blokes out here, they respect what they find. Life can be a battle out here, and people respect that. You know?"

Charlie rumbled a thoughtful agreement. Nicholas subsided, though he looked unsettled. Robin was gaping at the potential for drama.

They remained silent almost right through to Charleville.

three

Back in Brisbane, they did the usual tourist things with Robin. They drove down to the Gold Coast beaches a few times, they wandered through the South Bank gardens, window-shopped in the city, browsed the markets, visited the Koala Sanctuary. Denise, Vittorio and the girls joined them for lunch on the paddle steamer that ran down the river, before heading into town to indulge in the most extravagant ice cream sundaes known to humanity.

Dave encouraged Robin to try abseiling at Kangaroo Point Cliffs, but he suspected he was on a losing wicket there, even after Nicholas gamely said he'd try it, too. "We owe it to David," Nicholas pointed out. "After all, we made him take us to the art gallery."

At which Robin just snorted.

"Don't tell your Uncle Nicholas," Dave stage-whispered, "but I actually kind of enjoyed that." Which was true, if only because Nicholas had made for an interesting and surprisingly knowledgeable guide, who knew more about the history of Australian art than Dave had even guessed at.

Dave had an Outback trip planned for late July with a family who wanted to fossick for opals, and another trip later on with a bunch of blokes who were more into pubs and off-roading, but Dave had delegated his other two business bookings to the retired couple who helped him out when needed. At least Robin was keen on the idea of him and Nicholas coming along on the fossicking trip, but otherwise he seemed content to simply hang out.

More to the point, Robin was perfectly happy to keep company with Nicholas. It was obvious Robin was still in love with Nicholas – and when Dave thought back to being eighteen and in love and on his summer holidays, he could perfectly understand Robin's lazy contentment.

One warm afternoon they were all three hanging out in the shade on the back veranda. Dave was stretched out on a recliner with his current Patrick O'Brian novel, while Robin was curled up on the swing chair beside his beloved Nicholas. Robin had been listening to his music, though he'd only had one earbud in, and Nicholas had been browsing through one of his glossier academic journals, but even such pleasing demands as these had been put aside. The backyard stretched before them, looking particularly green and lush, and when the leaves of the banana palms stirred in the occasional breeze they sounded as beautiful as the patter of gentle rain.

There was certainly a sense shared among the three men, Dave thought, of all being very right with the world. So it was no surprise or interruption when Robin softly announced, "I love it here. I really do."

Nicholas smiled broadly, and said, "I'm glad. I love it here, too."

"I can see why you had to come live here."

"It was David," Nicholas said. "David belongs here, and I belong with David." Nicholas exchanged a solemnly happy glance with Dave, before adding to Robin, "I didn't *want* to leave you all behind, you know."

"I know." Robin sighed, and the quiet returned for a while. Until Robin tentatively began again, "I was thinking …"

"Yes?" Nicholas prompted.

"I was thinking that … maybe I should defer my enrolment at Oxford, and spend some time here with you instead."

Nicholas's expression slipped from tranquil to troubled in a moment, though he seemed to be trying to remain calm on the surface. "Were you?" he asked in fairly neutral tones.

"Yes. Lots of people take a gap year before starting uni, you know?"

"They do," Nicholas allowed. "Usually there's some … purpose to it, though."

"Like there's any better purpose for me than being with *you*," Robin returned.

Dave tensed a little, and sensed that Nicholas did, too. That was about as blatant as Robin had ever been – in words anyway. For some reason it all seemed much safer if it remained unspoken, or at most a subject for teasing, no matter how well known.

Eventually Nicholas said, "Well, let's see how you're feeling in a couple of months –"

"Of *course* I'll still feel the same –"

"About the gap year, I mean. Your grandfather is coming over to collect you, remember? If you can convince *him* to leave you here rather than take you back to Oxford, then I won't get in your way. You can tell him you have a home here with us."

"Thank you!" Robin cried, sitting up to look at Nicholas with a bright smile as if it were all already agreed. "Oh, *thank you*, Nicholas!"

Dave snorted. Nicholas's father was a lovely guy, and particularly fond of Nicholas, but Dave had seen him in Formidable Mode. "If you're serious, Robin, you'd better come up with a better reason than just hanging out with us. I don't think Richard's going to be very impressed. *I* wouldn't want to have to argue your case for you."

Robin barely spared Dave a glance.

For some reason, Dave persisted, when really he knew he should be dissuading the young man. "What are you gonna be studying at uni? I know I should know already, but these things tend to go right over my head. Maybe you can do a year's study here that would be – well, relevant."

"I doubt it," said Robin. "I'm doing PPE."

"You're such a frightful snob!" Nicholas told Robin – before he took pity on Dave and explained, "PPE: Philosophy, Politics and Economics." He added wryly, "Robin's going to be prime minister one day."

"Not of Australia, I take it."

"No," and Nicholas intoned, "Prime Minister of the United Kingdom of Great Britain and Northern Ireland."

Robin didn't care about being teased. He was sitting sideways on the chair now with his leg folded under him, focussed entirely and intensely on his uncle. "Nicholas," Robin said.

"Yes?"

It seemed that Robin was determined to finally lay all his cards out on the table. "You know I'm in love with you, Nicholas. You've always known, haven't you?"

Nicholas took a long moment with that, and then looked up at Robin with a troubled grimace. Eventually he began, "Maybe you are in love, my dear –"

"*Don't* patronise me!"

"– but being in love passes."

"It *won't* pass."

"I'm just trying to say – don't go making any life-changing decisions, all right, Robin? Let's wait and see how you feel when Father –"

"Oh, *wait and see*," Robin grumbled. "You're not so old, are you, that you can't remember being fed up to the back teeth with being told to *wait and see*?"

That won a reluctant quirk of a smile from Nicholas, but he didn't give an inch. "In any case, Robin," he steadily continued, "I'm with David, and always will be, and that's all there is to say about that."

"But that doesn't matter," Robin earnestly continued, glancing again at Dave –

"I assure you it matters very much indeed!" Nicholas retorted.

"No, I mean – David, *you* don't mind, do you? Me being in love with Nicholas? It's not like anything's ever gonna happen."

Dave slowly swung around to put his feet on the ground and sat up to face the others more directly. He wasn't entirely confident about what to say for the best, but then he took another breath and gave it a shot. "It's not that I *mind*, but I think you'd be a lot happier if you loved someone who could love you back –"

"But he does."

"– in the same way." Dave sighed. "You know what I'm trying to say, Robin."

"But he does love me, and he lets me cuddle him, and he smiles at me, and I don't need anything more than that."

"Well," said Dave, "it's not that I don't understand about the smiles."

"So, you don't mind sharing, right?" Robin persisted. "Because, you know, he still loves you and cuddles you and smiles at you. It's not like I'm taking anything away from what you want."

Dave frowned, and looked to Nicholas for a way forward. "I'm stumped," he said.

Nicholas seemed more troubled than ever. "That's not all there is to love, Robin –"

"It's all I want."

"– and you'll forgive us for wanting you to have someone in your life who'll return your love in kind."

"I don't want to have sex with you!" Robin blurted. Into the silence, he continued in somewhat more reasonable tones, "I don't want to have sex with anyone."

Nicholas rubbed at his forehead in a way that caused Dave deep misgivings. "*What?*" Nicholas asked sharply.

"I'm – I'm –"

Oh God, thought Dave. *He's coming out. Just not the way we expected.*

"I'm asexual, you see." Robin looked from one to the other of them, pale and right on the edge. "I'm just not into all that."

"But," Nicholas gritted out, "you said you're in love with me."

"You can be into love and not into sex."

Nicholas scowled, and started massaging his own scalp, digging his fingers in as if desperate to relieve the tension.

"Nicholas –" Dave said.

"I'm all right," he replied, before turning back to Robin. "How do you know? Have you tried?"

Robin scowled right back. "Did you have to 'try' before you knew you were gay?"

"No, but you're – forgive me for saying so, but you're very *young*, Robin, and –"

"I'm eighteen! How old were you? You said you've always known. Well, I've always known, too. Even if I didn't have a word for it."

"No," said Nicholas. "Just – no."

Robin stared at him, somehow going paler still. The kid was terrified. "*Please*, Nicholas …"

"What?" Nicholas looked as if he were under siege. "What is it you want?"

"Just to *understand* –"

"You want me to understand? I don't even think *you* understand!"

"I do. I do. I know who I am, just like you did."

Nicholas groaned and shook his head, his gaze darting about as if desperate for inspiration. He looked at Dave, and looked away – and then realised. "You know what, Robin? David didn't know. When he was eighteen, he thought he was entirely straight. I just think you should allow for the fact that you might be … mistaken."

Robin turned to consider Dave with an anxious grimace, as if both needing and dreading to hear more.

Oh God. "Well …" Dave began, slowly and carefully. "Nicholas is right, as far as that goes. I was with Denise when I was your age. And I loved her, I really did. I thought I'd always be … with Denise. But looking back … When she admired other men, I always had an opinion. I thought it was like appreciating a beautiful sunset, you know? I thought I was just open-minded. I think we both … had a bit of a thing for Pete Murray. It was only later I realised that … straight guys don't think like that. Not even about Pete. Even when I met Nicholas, it took me ages to realise I'm actually bisexual. I guess I was a bit …" What Aussie man would ever want to admit this? "I was a bit innocent, you know? Even a bit naïve, maybe."

"Innocent," Nicholas said with a nod, fastening onto this word. "You need to live more of your life, Robin, before you go deciding on labels like – Well. Deciding on fundamental things like that."

Robin had turned back to gape at Nicholas. "I thought *you* would understand, Nicholas. Even if no one else does, I thought you'd be the one who'd let me be who I am."

Nicholas scoffed a little. "Into love and not into sex? How does that even work?"

It had been a difficult enough situation as it was. Now Dave felt a cold stir of foreboding. "Nicholas –"

"I know *you're* into sex, Uncle Nicholas."

"Yes, I am," he returned in tones that Dave felt were a bit too defiant for such a sensitive conversation with young Robin.

"That doesn't mean everyone else has to be."

"Nicholas," said Dave. "Maybe you should give Robin the benefit of the doubt. At least for now. He's obviously put a lot of thought into this –"

Nicholas stared hard at Dave – and then dropped his head into his hands, and dug his fingers into his temples. He obviously had a headache. Dave's cold sense of foreboding deepened.

"Uncle Nicholas –" Robin began.

Dave was on his feet even before Nicholas was –

But in the event, Nicholas just walked past him, holding out a hand to indicate Dave needn't follow. "It's all right," he said. Dave had learned to trust him when he said that. "I'm all right." He was heading inside.

"Uncle Nicholas –"

"Sorry. I can't handle this right now." And Nicholas was through the French windows into the relative darkness of the house, sliding the screen-door closed behind him until it shut with a quiet *snick*.

Robin sat back down again.

So did Dave. They both stared at the wooden decking of the veranda, and then exchanged a cautious glance as if each checking the other was okay. Dave would rather be with Nicholas, taking care of him, but he couldn't abandon Robin. Not when Robin had just been rejected by the man he was in love with. "Are you all right?" Dave eventually asked.

Robin looked at him, pale yet steady. "All right enough. Is Nicholas – ?"

"He'll be fine. He'll drink his water-and-lime, and take a couple of pills for his headache. Maybe he'll read or have a nap. He'll be fine."

A solemn nod acknowledged all this. Then Robin sighed, settled back in the swing chair, and stared off into the abundant greenery of the yard. He snubbed a toe against the decking and pushed the chair back, and then let it swing in a gentle arc to and fro, to and fro.

Dave watched him. Robin had always seemed relatively young to him. It didn't help that whenever Nicholas was around, Robin turned as giddy as a bandicoot, but even so. Dave could have sworn he himself had been far more grown-up at eighteen, even if he had been an innocent in some ways. After all, at eighteen Dave had been working full-time with his dad, and Denise had moved into this house with them as Dave's partner. Dave had thought he'd known everything about how his life would be.

Well, Dave had been wrong about a lot of that – but looking at Robin now, Dave could see a maturity behind the youthful face, and a core of … certainty. A calm confidence at the heart of him. An underlying self-possession. And *that* reminded Dave of Nicholas. If only the two of them could avoid falling out over this, perhaps Nicholas would come to see that, too.

"What are you thinking, Uncle David?"

"I was thinking that … everything's going to be just fine."

"Good," said Robin. "That's good."

In the darkness that night, Dave surfaced from vague dreams as Nicholas's embrace tightened, as his hold on Dave became a grasp. "All right?" Dave muttered. "Nicholas?"

"Yes," Nicholas reassured him, though his breath was harsh in his throat as if he'd been running *hard*. His hands became demanding, and he grappled Dave under him, though he said, "Please –"

"Course," Dave said, already welcoming him with arms and thighs. It was so dark, Dave hardly even knew whether his eyes were open or not, but they definitely closed as Nicholas pressed his face into Dave's throat, as he bit at him and gnawed, and rumbled a growl that shuddered through Dave. Nicholas's cock hadn't caught up with the rest of him yet, but as he rubbed himself against Dave's cock and balls, he soon hardened.

"David?" Nicholas asked.

"Not the whole hog, yeah?"

Nicholas grunted assent, and instead thrust up against him, hard and hot now and the friction just on the right side of bearable. Dave came almost without being aware of it, the dreams slipping through into reality and the pleasure pushing him back into a sweet daze. Nicholas had to work for his release, his cock sliding through the stickiness of Dave's spunk, his mouth alternating bites and kisses. Dave ran his hands down Nicholas's back, soothing him, maybe helping, maybe not. But then at last Nicholas came, and he collapsed into Dave's embrace, and Dave rocked him gently, voicing an incoherent murmur on every breath, until eventually Nicholas fell asleep.

Early the next morning, Charlie rang.

four

"Mate," Charlie said when Dave answered the phone.

Dave instinctively responded to the slight edge of worry to Charlie's tone. "What is it? What's wrong?"

There was a brief silence which Dave knew better than to interrupt. Then Charlie said, "I heard from people that Ted Walinski, that surveyor, has been asking questions in Cunnamulla."

Dave let a beat go by. "What kind of questions?"

"He has a lump of what he says is hematite, and he's showing it to the locals, asking if they know where it came from."

"Hematite being …"

"Iron ore."

Dave frowned over that, trying to ignore the sense of dread like lead in his stomach. "Are you sure?" He turned to find Robin sitting at the table in the family room, apparently playing some kind of game on his phone. "Robin, I've got an old geology textbook in the spare room. Would you fetch it for me?"

Robin didn't budge, but asked helpfully enough, "What do you want to know?"

"I want to check that hematite is the kind of iron ore that the mining companies are after."

A nod from Robin, as he swiped out of the game and started tapping away at the virtual keyboard.

Dave turned back to the phone. "Charlie." He took a breath. "Does that mean he's found the waterhole?"

"Walinski? Nah. But he's saying the rock came from west of town, out beyond the Aboriginal reserve."

Which caused more frowning. "But if he hasn't found the waterhole, then how does he know that's where the rock came from?"

"Guess he found it in the general area, and can't find his way further in, and you've made him curious." Charlie huffed a sigh, and Dave could perfectly visualise him round-faced with breath-filled cheeks. "It's not the actual Dreaming site he's interested in."

"No, but it's bad enough, isn't it?"

"It *is* bad," Robin chipped in.

Dave turned to face him, and held the phone in his direction, too, hoping that Charlie would hear. "Go on, then."

"Wikipedia says that iron ore containing hematite is what the mining companies like best, because it can go directly into the furnaces without any processing. They call it 'natural ore'. And it gets worse," Robin added.

By then Nicholas had come through from the lounge room, and was hovering anxiously. Charlie prompted, "Go on," in Dave's ear, which Dave passed on with an encouraging nod.

"It says that most reserves of natural ore have been used up already, or the ones that are accessible, anyway. So I guess that means," Robin said, looking at Dave with widened gaze, "they'll be really keen."

An edgy silence grew.

Nicholas sat down beside Robin, and tried to read the entry Robin had displayed on his phone, but really Nicholas couldn't tear his attention away from Dave.

Eventually Charlie said, "I'm heading down there, mate. To Cunnamulla. I'll see what's happening."

"I'll meet you there," said Dave.

Nicholas nodded, and stood up again. "I'll get us packed."

"Are you sure? We've got that fossicking trip coming up. Maybe you two should pace yourselves."

"No, we'll come," said Nicholas.

Dave lifted his chin at Robin. "It's a ten-hour drive, mate. You sure you're up for it?"

"We're coming, Uncle David," said Robin, also standing, like he meant business.

"We'll see you tonight, Charlie," said Dave.

"Take the Goondiwindi road," Charlie advised.

Dave didn't even bother asking why. "Will do. See ya, then."

"See ya."

"Shall we pack for a couple of nights?" Nicholas asked. "Or more, just in case?"

By the time they reached Cunnamulla that evening, there was already a buzz in the air. It was soon clear that the local community had been quick to extrapolate from a lump of reddish rock to a huge investment in the area from a well-funded mining company.

Dave, Nicholas and Robin found Charlie at the second of the pubs they tried. He was sitting back in a chair at a small table, with his arms crossed, looking as if his thoughts were miles away. Dave murmured a greeting, but when Charlie didn't respond, the three of them simply sat, and worked out what they would have for dinner. By the time Dave had been to the bar to order – including steak, potatoes and veg for Charlie – and returned with two beers and two lemonades, he'd overheard enough in any case.

"You know what happens to wages when the mining boys come to town?" one bloke asked his companion, purely rhetorically.

"They go through the roof, mate," was the complacent response.

"Mate, they'd go through the roof of a ten-storey building."

"So do prices, though," someone else chipped in.

"Reckon I can live with that."

"There's none ever come this far west, though," another guy fretfully observed.

"They'd come for 'shipping ore'. That's the quality stuff!"

"We've already got the railway," the first bloke reassured everyone in hearing distance, "and the airport, too."

Dave sat down again next to Nicholas with a sigh, and his husband gazed back at him worriedly.

"How long until dinner's ready?" asked Robin.

"Won't be long, mate. Ten, fifteen minutes."

"David," said Nicholas, leaning forward to speak quietly. "David, what about the butterflies?"

"They'll be all right. We'll do whatever it takes, Nicholas."

"David –"

"Maybe nothing will come of this anyway," Dave said, trying to remind himself of that fact. "And even if it did, it'll be obvious to everyone that we have to protect the butterflies. Quite apart from the – the rest."

He hadn't managed to quite say 'Dreamtime', because one of the younger blokes had come up to the table. "Did you hear?" he asked – not waiting for an answer before he continued. "They've found iron ore west of here."

"Yeah, we picked up on that," Dave replied in what he hoped were neutral tones.

"Apparently it's somewhere near where you guys go camping, you know?"

They were all four of them silent, which probably wasn't the best response.

"Is that why you guys are here again? Gonna see if you can help find it?"

"Oh! No … No …" Dave tilted his head, trying to gather his thoughts. Lying didn't come easy, but he wasn't sure yet about where to draw the line between concealing and revealing the truth. "We're, uh – We've got a fossicking trip coming up, out Yowah way. Thought we'd scout the place. See if Charlie'll join us."

"Sure. Yowah nuts!" the young bloke responded enthusiastically.

Robin's eyebrows shot into his hairline. "Yowah nuts … ? Sounds painful."

"They're opals," Dave explained to Robin. "You find them inside rocks," he indicated the size and rough shape with a cupped hand. "Reddish-brown rocks that look like large nuts – the sort you eat. Never mind that," he said as Nicholas's smirk grew. "Or maybe they look like gumnuts, I dunno. They're round or ellip- … egg-shaped."

"How do you know the opals are in there, then?"

"You learn what to look for. You develop an eye for it."

"Cool!" Robin said, lighting up. "Oh, I'm going to find the most beautiful opal in all the world …"

Charlie finally stirred out of his reverie. "Opals? Count me in."

The four of them ate their dinner in relative silence, each of them tired or downcast or both. Finally, once they were done and the table was cleared, Charlie leaned in and offered, "Like you said: maybe nothing will come of it."

But Dave shook his head. "We can't take the risk. Not on this." He pushed in closer, too, leaning his elbows on the table, trying to look casual. "Look. Can we head out to the reserve tomorrow, and maybe – finally – start a conversation with the Elders?"

Charlie pursed his lips. "It's all just been talk, hasn't it, and a few locals with dollar signs in their eyes."

"I know, but if something's gonna happen, then we want to stay one step ahead, right?"

A shrug from those eloquent shoulders, but then Charlie said, "Yeah, all right." A few minutes later he tipped a farewell nod to them, and headed out.

Dave sighed. "Come on, then," he said to the others. "Let's get checked in to the hotel."

Dave and Charlie had been here many times before. Once or twice a year, they came to the reserve, sat in a circle with the Elders and anyone else who happened to be there that day, and they spoke when they were spoken to but otherwise held their peace.

No one ever raised the matter of Charlie knowing the Dreaming songs for the waterhole when actually he shouldn't, nor about him having had the audacity to then pass them on to a white fella. Charlie had gone on his own to tell them that news, seven years ago now, and had reported that the circle of men and women had all talked and talked until everyone understood, and then they'd fallen quiet as they'd pondered the situation. There had been no conclusions reached, no judgement given.

Dave had gone to the reserve with Charlie a tactful month or so later, half-knowing that he should be forbidden from the sacred site, half-expecting to be quizzed or harassed about it all, but of course that wasn't the Murri way. Everyone still seemed to be taking it in and trying to work out what to think about the matter. Later he wondered if the Elders had decided on a 'wait and see' approach. None of the Murri spoke against him and Charlie keeping the songs alive, or at least not in Dave's hearing. Perhaps they, like Charlie, took the pragmatic view that the important thing was that the songs be sung, that the Earth's energies be renewed, that the relationship between land and people be maintained.

And so, in the 'eternal now' or 'everywhen' of Indigenous thinking, the Elders were pondering – and in Dave's white-fella view, time passed, and the whole thing became a fait accompli. Which was fine by Dave, and if it could have lasted through decades until it was finally time to find someone else to learn the songs, that would have been great. But it seemed that gubbah business – white-fella stuff – was going to intrude whether they were ready or not.

That day, Nicholas and Robin went to join the sociable mob which was gathered in front of the local store. They were soon sharing a drink and a jovial yarn with a range of people of all ages, all colours. After a few moments to make sure they were going to be okay, however, Dave and Charlie headed for the quieter group who were sitting in a loose circle under the shade of a huge red gum. There was a space that would fit the two of them and, as they approached, one of the Elders nodded – whether that was coincidental or not, Dave nodded a greeting, and he and Charlie settled cross-legged on the ground.

It was peacefully quiet in the circle, at just enough distance from the other mob that they couldn't make out specific words amidst the general talk – at least not until there was a scandalised "No way!" from Robin, which caused much merriment. Dave could make out Nicholas's laugh amidst the rest, which made him smile, and he exchanged a fond glance with Charlie.

Eventually, when there was a lull in the thoughts and meandering words of the group, Dave quietly asked, "May I talk to you, please? About the waterhole, about the Dreaming site where the Barcoo grunter sleeps." He didn't use the place's proper name, or the Ancestor's, even in this company. Neither did he have to explain further. It wasn't as if they didn't all know, even if they'd never spoken to him about it.

The lull became something more attentive, and a few of the others exchanged quiet words between themselves. After a while Dave sensed that he was welcome to continue, and Charlie murmured, "Yeah, go on."

"It's a very beautiful place," Dave surprised himself by saying. "It's precious. The water in the pool … it's like a jewel. The colours are so vivid … The layers of rock are red, and there's the green of the eucalypts, the gold of the wattle when it flowers. There are the butterflies, the most fantastic blue butterflies. My husband found them." He indicated Nicholas, though of course everyone there already knew about Dave and Nicholas. "The butterflies are unique, he thinks – but it's not only that. They're part of the Dreaming story about the waterhole, about the Ancestor who sleeps there and the Ancestor he loved who came down from the sky. It's a … a really incredible place."

He stumbled to a halt, having completely failed to reach the nub of the matter.

But then one of Elders nodded, and said, "We know you love the land."

Dave almost let out a gasp at that, and his eyes prickled embarrassingly. He hadn't expected to ever hear such a thing. Not ever. "Thank you," he said, not daring to even glance at Charlie for fear of the tears really welling up.

After a moment Dave considered what to say next. Even after such an acknowledgement, he wasn't going to ask permission to continue as custodian of the site, and risk a refusal. He had better pass on the news first, and then see where that left them.

"Look," Dave said, cutting right to the chase now, in his white-fella way. "The rock there – I think it's so red because it contains iron ore. And now a surveyor is trying to find it, and everyone in town is getting all excited, expecting a mining company to follow."

A silence fell after this great blurt. Dave looked around at faces that seemed even more enigmatic than usual. Charlie was looking pensive.

Eventually one of the men commented, "If they bring jobs and money, that's worth getting excited about."

"Well, yes," Dave agreed, his gut sinking. It was a fair point. "But I'm concerned that – that we make sure the Dreaming site isn't disturbed. And that the butterflies are safe."

"Yes," said one of the Elders, the one who'd nodded a welcome to Dave when he and Charlie first arrived. Dave didn't know his Indigenous name, but he went by the nickname 'Thursday'.

"Thank you, Thursday," Dave said. "I guess I just need to know that – if we have to make this official somehow – you'll support Charlie about him knowing the songs."

"No, mate," Charlie protested. "It's you that belongs there."

Dave turned to stare at him. *Are you kidding … ?* "Mate, no one's gonna take that seriously!"

Charlie put on his most mulish expression, and insisted as he'd insisted before, "Old man grunter chose you." Then he kind of hunkered down inside himself as if withdrawing from all further discussion.

"I'll back you up, mate," Dave said, "but you've got to be the front man, if push comes to shove."

Silence.

Dave sighed, and fell into a ponder of his own. It wasn't that he had any firm plans yet, because he hardly knew what they'd be facing, but his initial sketches were already falling apart.

After a while, though, Thursday said, "You can speak for us, Dave. You can figure out what has to be done, and you can speak for us."

"I can?" he asked, somewhat flabbergasted.

"When it's time for us to speak, we will."

"Good. That's good. Wow." Dave hunkered down into himself, too, suddenly having a whole lot of rethinking to do. But he didn't neglect to say, "Thank you."

When he and Charlie finally got up to go, it wasn't only Thursday who nodded a farewell.

In town the next day, Dave ran into Ted Walinski as he, Nicholas and Robin were walking back from the shops. Part of Dave wondered if he should just push past the man on the grounds that sometimes discretion really is the better part of valour. Within the moment it took to reach him, though, Dave had decided that it was time to start taking a stand. "Morning," he said, pausing on the pavement in the shade of an awning.

"Morning, Mr Taylor," Walinski replied, stopping likewise, and nodding a genial greeting to them all.

"It's Goring Taylor now," Dave said.

"Right you are."

"Look," said Dave. "What are you up to?"

Walinski took a long cool look at him, and then glanced down at the pavement – almost as if miming a spit – before meeting his gaze again. "I'm doing some surveying for Mrs Wilson. Trying to establish her easterly boundaries."

"Henrietta Wilson?" She owned the larger of the two ranches on the far side of the waterhole.

"Yes. It's been dry, as you know. She wants to use more of her land to run her cattle, but it'll need fencing."

Dave considered the man. That was all fine, as far as it went, though the further east Henri Wilson pushed, the closer she'd get to the waterhole. Dave had to wonder if that was coincidence or not. He let that be, however, and tried another tack. "What about this rock you've been showing around? Getting everyone excited about mining rights."

Walinski started digging in his jeans pocket as soon as Dave said 'rock', and held it out to him. "Here, then."

Dave didn't take the thing, but peered at it, as did Nicholas and Robin. It did look very much like the rock in the cliffs that surrounded the waterhole. In fact, Dave had to suppress an instinctive *zing* running through him – though whether that was recognition or simple anxiety, he had no idea.

"Does it look familiar?" Walinski asked.

"Mate, it looks like a rock." Dave stood tall again, though he couldn't help crossing his arms. "Lot o' years gone by since my high school geology class."

Robin pitched in, perhaps hoping to confuse the issue. "It's not one of those Yowah nuts you were telling me about, Uncle David? You said they were a kind of reddish colour."

"No, mate, definitely not one of those." He asked Walinski, "So, what's your interest? You working for one of the mining companies now, or you gonna be selling to the highest bidder?"

Walinski shrugged, and quipped, "That's 'commercial in confidence', Mr Goring Taylor."

Dave let out a sigh. "So, this is really happening, isn't it?" He glanced at Nicholas, who nodded, with a tense expression on his face that Dave found nigh on unbearable. "Look, Mr Walinski," Dave said, turning to face the man square on. "There's a Dreamtime site out there, and there's a unique species of butterfly that Nicholas has written up in his … you know, academic journals and such. So, there's going to be some land that's off-limits."

A slow nod met this assertion, and after a long moment, Walinski said, "Thank you for telling me." He let a beat go by, and then lifted the rock between them again. "So, do you know where this is from?"

Dave took another breath, but then said, "I'll have to think about that."

"Fair enough."

"If I can help, I'll get back to you."

Walinski nodded, and held out his hand to shake. "Thank you, Mr Goring Taylor."

Dave shook the man's hand, more from a sense of fairness than an overwhelming sense of fellow feeling. And then they parted.

Dave, Nicholas and Robin continued back to the hotel in silence, though Dave sensed that Nicholas was barely restraining himself from speaking.

Finally, once they were in the privacy of the Land Cruiser heading back to Brisbane, Nicholas said, "The butterflies –"

"I know. I promise: we'll do whatever we have to, right?"

"Yes."

Dave glanced at his husband, really not liking to see anxiety so dark on Nicholas's brow. "You've done everything you can to document them, right? I mean, you've written articles, had them listed or – um, registered or whatever it is you do, yeah?"

"Yes." Nicholas returned his glance, a little rueful. "The only thing I couldn't do was really pinpoint the location. Though I described it as well as I was able."

"Of course, yeah."

A moment dragged by. Until finally Nicholas said, "Maybe we're the ones who need a surveyor."

Dave frowned over that, but he had to acknowledge, "Maybe you're right."

five

They arrived home late that night. Robin was hungry, so Dave began gathering the makings for an omelette, while Robin sat and shared his attention between watching Dave and checking his phone.

When Nicholas appeared, however, Robin put the phone down. Nicholas was looking a bit tired and careworn, but not unhappy. He diverted to press a grateful kiss to Dave's temple before going to sit opposite Robin – and then they were all quiet for a long moment.

Finally Robin said, "Uncle Nicholas –"

"Yes?" Nicholas prompted with the slightest of smiles, which seemed to be all he could muster.

"You know what we talked about … about me, I mean."

"Yes." Nicholas sat up, and leaned forward. Dropped his face into his hands and rubbed hard, as if trying to wake himself up. When he looked at Robin again, he said, "I'm sorry. Events kind of overtook us, didn't they?"

Robin took a breath. "I just want to know that we're … all right."

Nicholas put a bit more effort into his smile. "Of course we're all right, Robin. I love you no matter what. We both do. Always will."

"You don't understand, though, do you?"

"Does that matter?" Nicholas sat back again, turning a tad disgruntled despite himself. "Isn't unconditional love good enough any more?"

Robin's cheeks coloured in chagrin, and he picked up his phone again though he didn't look at it.

Dave had finished chopping the shallots and bacon, so he put them on to sauté – at a low heat, just in case the meal needed to be delayed.

Eventually Nicholas burst out, "I just think you're missing out on something – something marvellous. Maybe even –" He glanced at Dave, and seemed to grow in conviction. "Yes. One of the best bits of life."

"I'm perfectly happy being a virgin," Robin steadily replied, "and I probably always will be. It's not going to be, like … something I regret."

"But how do you *know* if you haven't tried?"

"How do you know you don't want to go to bed with a girl?"

"That's really *not* the same thing. I wish you'd stop trying to compare my situation to yours."

When Robin didn't reply, Dave put down the cheese he was grating, and tried, "Nicholas, perhaps you can just be happy that Robin is happy."

"How can he be happy at the *lack* of something?" Nicholas demanded.

"Well, I don't know. But it seems like he is. Doesn't it?"

Nicholas considered Dave. Considered Robin. Finally sighed, and gave in with a nod. "All right, yes. Fine. Robin, I'm happy if you're happy."

"I'm happy," Robin said, though in a very small voice.

"That's good, then," Nicholas concluded. "That's great." He got up and went to lean over Robin to give him a hug.

"Thank you, Uncle Nicholas."

"No worries," said Nicholas – which made Dave smile, as it was such an Aussie expression. But then Nicholas stood, and headed towards the hallway. "I'm going to bed," he announced, with an apologetic smile for Dave. "I'm sorry, that smells delicious, but I'm really not hungry."

"No worries," Dave said in turn, smiling fondly at his husband as he and Robin wished each other goodnight. "See you in a bit." Then Nicholas was gone, and Dave turned to Robin. "You're still hungry, I hope?"

"Too right, I am!"

"That's grand." And Dave poured the beaten eggs into the pan, where they sizzled in a most satisfying manner.

"I have an idea," Nicholas announced the next morning over breakfast.

Dave and Robin looked at him expectantly.

"It might not only be the butterflies that are unique. When I took a sample of the wattle to one of my colleagues in Flora, she couldn't identify it for certain. She said it was very close to two different species, but couldn't decide between them. So that's how I wrote it up, and I never really pursued it further. But maybe it's time."

Dave nodded, but asked, "Time for what?"

"Well … maybe to bring back some proper samples for Lisa to analyse – if she has the resources. Though I'm sure she'd find a way to make it happen, wouldn't she? If it might be a new species of *Acacia*, I mean."

"She didn't pursue it before, though?"

Nicholas tilted his head in a quibble. "I may have over-emphasised the secret side of it being a sacred site. But it's been isolated for so long – the wattle, I mean – and in a symbiotic relationship of sorts with the butterflies. Whatever it used to be may well have evolved into something else by now."

"Symbiotic?" Dave said. "That makes it sound a bit – weird."

"Well, I just mean, given there don't seem to be any other insects around, and it's so sheltered there, it must be the butterflies that pollinate it. In return, it provides them with shelter and sustenance – and so on, and so on. It's this whole …"

"Great Circle of Life," Robin chipped in.

Nicholas laughed. "Yes, I was going to try for something more original, but that's it exactly."

Dave smiled at them both, and once the laughter had quietened, he said, "Would she come out on a trip, do you think, to see the wattle at the waterhole?"

"Oh," said Nicholas.

"Be better to see it in place, wouldn't it? In its natural habitat? And you don't want to take too much away as a sample. It's not like there's a lot of it, as it is."

"Oh, well. That would be great, and I'm sure she'd love to. But what about keeping the waterhole secret?"

"I've just been thinking, old man grunter won't mind me sharing it a bit wider. In fact, I'm thinking maybe it's time. And anyway, the place keeps its own secrets. We're still the only ones who've actually managed to find it, since Charlie's friend died."

"*You're* the one who finds it," Nicholas corrected him, "each and every time. All right, I'll talk to her today, and see what she thinks. Robin," he added, turning towards the young man. "Do you want to come to the university with me for the day? Shall we give David a break from all the Goring dramatics?"

"He's probably earned it," Robin agreed.

Dave just laughed.

Dave had business to pursue, in any case. He'd made an appointment for an initial interview with a lawyer at the Native Title Services organisation that covered the Cunnamulla region, and what with the fossicking trip coming up, he'd pushed to make it sooner rather than later.

So that afternoon Dave headed into the city, dressed in a proper shirt and trousers, and ended up sitting across a desk from a man of about Dave's own age or a bit younger, named Martin Bandjara. The place was obviously busy, with the phones in the main office ringing amidst ongoing chatter, and Martin's desk piled high with paperwork. He seemed genuinely interested in taking the time to engage with Dave, though, and when he asked, "How can I help you?" he seemed to really want to know.

"I'm interested," said Dave – "well, it's early days yet, but I'm interested in making a claim for Native Title."

"And you're acting on behalf of … ?"

"Myself, really. Or the Dreaming site, I guess. Basically, I'm looking to protect a Dreaming site."

Martin let a beat go by, and then he said, "Forgive me. But you look to be – white."

Dave huffed a breath that might almost have been a laugh. "I'm a white fella, yes. I realise this is probably a bit … unusual."

"You have an Indigenous predecessor, perhaps? A grandparent or great-grandparent?"

"Not that I know of. My dad's family were English; he emigrated, and I was born here. My mum's family were Irish and English originally, but they've been out here for generations."

"Ah, so there's a possibility one of them might have married an Indigenous person, or had a child with one, at least?"

Dave shook his head, beginning to realise that Martin's persistence didn't bode well for his case. "No, I really don't think so."

"The family might have … hidden the fact."

"I realise that times have changed, and for the better, but I don't think we've ever been the kind of people who would have felt ashamed of it."

Martin nodded. "Then – sorry – but what's your connection with this Dreaming site you mentioned?"

Dave told the story again, of how Charlie's friend had been the last of his tribe, and he'd passed the songs and stories to Charlie rather than let them be lost.

"And there's no chance that your mate Charlie has some kind of family connection with the tribe? Anything at all?"

"I wouldn't have thought so … No. I mean, that's the point, isn't it? His friend was already crossing the line in passing the songs to Charlie. And now Charlie seems to think I'm more entitled to them than he is."

Martin frowned in confusion. "Why exactly is that? I mean … if you don't mind me asking."

So Dave explained how Charlie hadn't been able to find the sacred site, but Dave had; and how Charlie had become convinced that Dave was the rightful custodian of the waterhole, especially once he'd discovered that Dave had been born in Cunnamulla, and conceived nearby as well. "So, you see," Dave concluded, "I've kind of inherited this in a … well, in a *spiritual* sense, yeah?" His face flamed. This was worse than talking about sex or love. "Not in the sense of bloodlines."

Martin considered him thoughtfully for long moments. Finally he said, "You seem sincere about this."

"Yeah, I am," he replied in easy tones despite the fact his face was still bright red.

"And you actually go there and perform the rituals every now and then?"

"Yes, of course. We haven't missed even one. Sometimes Charlie comes, too. Sometimes I go on my own. Well, with my – husband."

Martin didn't blink at that latest revelation. After a moment, he simply said, "Mr Goring Taylor –"

"Dave."

"Dave. I don't know what to tell you. It's remarkable that you've taken this responsibility so seriously. But – the Native Title Act is designed to recognise the traditional owners of the land, and their biological descendants."

"Ah."

"They are required to have continued to practise the traditional customs associated with that area, just as you have done, but –"

"No, I get it," said Dave, hardly able to bear hearing any more. "I've been naïve again, haven't I?"

"Not naïve," Martin protested. "In an ideal world –"

"Okay, so there's no chance," Dave concluded heavily.

"I'm afraid the right to claim, as the law currently stands, would have extinguished with the death of the last member of that tribe. If we tried to claim on the basis of a … a spiritual inheritance, then I doubt we'd get very far. To be honest, I'd love to try – to test the concept. But even if the Federal

Court took us seriously, they'd be wary of opening the floodgates. It would be setting a precedent for … well, for anyone to claim almost anything."

"I haven't invented this out of thin air," Dave argued. "I have a real concern for that waterhole. There's iron ore in the area, and a mining company has caught wind of it."

"You're …" Martin hesitated, and then asked almost apologetically, "You're interested in benefiting from the mining rights?"

"Not for myself, no, but if the Murri benefit from it, that's fine. I'm just wanting to protect that place."

Martin looked as if he were desperate to help. "Native Title isn't the answer," he concluded. "I only wish it were."

"Not even Charlie could claim Native Title?" Nicholas asked that evening.

"No biological connection," Dave confirmed. The three of them were sitting around the table in the family room, comparing notes about their days.

"So, what do we try next?"

Dave sighed. "The only real idea Martin and I came up with was to extend the reserve to include the area surrounding the waterhole. In which case, I can help, but it would have to be Thursday and his mob who make that happen."

"Well, that's all right, isn't it?"

"If it's made part of the reserve, then the people who live there will have a say in what happens, and they'll have the power to negotiate with a mining company. But there are plenty of locals who'll be happy for the work coming in – white fellas, Indigenous, or anyone else – and I can't say as I blame them. So I still feel like … well, like we need to do more to protect the waterhole itself, you know?"

"We might be able to help there. Do you want to tell him, Robin?"

Robin abruptly went pink, and stuttered a bit before saying, "Dr Munroe –"

"Lisa," Nicholas explained to Dave.

"– said she'd love to come out to the waterhole with us. She asked if she could bring her partner."

Nicholas grimaced. "I didn't mean *that* bit, Robin. I'm sorry, David.

I don't want to inundate the place with visitors."

"No, it's all right. I meant it about sharing."

"Go on, then, Robin," Nicholas said.

"W-w-well, Dr Munroe said she's very interested in the wattle, v-v-very interested indeed, and if it's rare then she can help protect it. And she asked if Nicholas had had the butterflies officially listed as 'Vulnerable'."

Nicholas was nodding along with this, sitting back in his seat and looking overly casual. "I've been a bit of an idiot not to have thought of this before. But the waterhole always seemed – so very secluded. Safe. And there's a sense there that nothing's changed for thousands of years, and probably won't for thousands yet."

"I know," Dave agreed. "Don't worry, I know what you mean. So, what's this vulnerable thing about?"

"We can nominate the *Ogyris davidi* species to be listed as 'Vulnerable' under the Nature Conservation Act. They're a textbook case, really." Nicholas counted off the points on his long fingers. "Their population is low; it's localised; it depends on a limited habitat; and that habitat might be at risk."

"Good," said Dave. "Okay. And once it's listed, what happens then?"

"Well, that opens up a number of possible activities, I suppose, but right now I'm thinking more about making it abundantly clear to any mining company that they can't just walk in and have everything their own way. If the waterhole is acknowledged as a Dreamtime site, in an Aboriginal reserve, with not one but two threatened species living there and nowhere else …" Nicholas grimaced and shrugged, throwing his hands out in a plea. "That would be a solid first step, wouldn't it?"

"It's perfect," said Dave. He got up and went to lean over Nicholas, and wrapped him up in a big grateful hug – which provoked a happy rumbling growl from Nicholas. "You're awesome," Dave said. "Both of you," he added, glancing across the table at Robin.

Dave expected to find Robin grimacing in distaste or rolling his eyes, but instead the young fella was looking rather indulgent. The probable reason seemed fairly obvious to Dave. "So …" he said, only loosening his hold on Nicholas enough so that they could all three converse. "Robin liked your mate Lisa, did he?"

Robin promptly blushed, but his smile was bright and uncomplicated.

"She was cool," he asserted. "She's like Uncle Nicholas, you know?"

Nicholas grinned. "I'm cool, am I? Wonders will never cease."

"You're pretty cool," Robin agreed. "But the thing I like is … you and Dr Munroe are both tall, dark and super intelligent."

Dave had to stand then, as his burst of laughter would have threatened Nicholas's eardrums.

"Oh my God …" Nicholas was drawling. "Robin has a type …"

Dave and Nicholas were curled up together under the doona that night. It was late and dark, and Robin was probably sound asleep, but nevertheless they whispered. "He's got a crush on Lisa … ?" Dave asked.

"Completely smitten," Nicholas confirmed, huffing a laugh under his breath.

"No change on the sexual side of things, though."

"I asked him afterwards, and he announced that he's asexual and bi-romantic." Nicholas shrugged. "I still don't understand, but he insists that romantic attraction and sexual attraction are two completely separate things."

"I think maybe he's right. I think maybe they are."

"Well," Nicholas responded – though how he could still sound tart while whispering, Dave had no idea. "Well, then you'd better explain it to me."

Dave let out a sigh. "I don't have the words to talk about that kind of thing, Nicholas."

"Try. You might surprise yourself."

"Anyway," Dave continued, letting his hands caress their way further down Nicholas's lithe body, "call me greedy, but I like having both mixed up together."

"Best thing in the world, having both," Nicholas agreed. He stretched out a little taller, pushed in a little closer.

Dave slipped a hand down to cup Nicholas's balls – and his cock, too, while it was still at rest – and he rolled the delicious handful in his palm. Nicholas groaned quietly and pushed closer still, wrapping his arms around Dave's shoulders. They bumped noses in the dark, but then they were kissing and mouthing hungrily. Soon Nicholas's cock was poking hard at Dave's wrist; he adjusted his hold slightly so he could rub the heel of his hand against it while still kneading his balls. A groan tore out of Nicholas, which Dave muffled with another kiss before gently shushing him.

"Quickly, then," Nicholas said, an insistent hand pushing down to wrap around Dave's cock. Nicholas shifted closer still, obviously wanting to wrap both their cocks up in one hand, as he'd liked to do ever since their first time together. Dave let go his own hold, but instead reached to bring Nicholas's leg up to hook around Dave's hip. By lifting up onto an elbow, Dave found he could reach down between Nicholas's thighs to tug at his balls from behind – which had Nicholas groaning again, and clinging on tight round his shoulders, round his cock. When Dave managed to grasp and rub at his own balls as well as Nicholas's, the orgasm hit them both like a lightning strike, and afterwards they lay welded together, panting and damp in each other's arms – and if they had after all made too much noise, in that moment Dave really didn't give a damn.

six

The clients for the fossicking trip were a well-off family who were quite happy to 'rough it' for a week, but wanted someone on hand who knew the ropes. It was hardly a challenging job, but Dave was perfectly happy to indulge them, especially as it meant he could give Nicholas and Robin a bit of a treat, working holiday though it was.

The three of them drove out to Cunnamulla again, and on the following morning went to meet the family who were flying in to Cunnamulla airport. Dave had talked to the father, Mike Baldry, on Skype a couple of times, so they recognised each other right away and shook hands heartily. Mike introduced his wife Suzanne, who seemed rather dauntingly elegant – until she grinned as broadly as her husband, and obliterated Dave's initial reservations. Their daughters Monica and Chloe were sixteen and fourteen years old respectively; the former was apparently going through the 'too cool for this' stage, but Robin and Chloe were soon nattering away excitedly.

Nicholas and Robin got the Baldrys' luggage neatly stowed in the back of the four-wheel drive Dave had rented for them, while Dave talked Mike through the controls, as he'd never driven anything beyond a regular sedan before. Not that they would be doing anything very challenging: it was sealed roads all the way to Yowah, and well-maintained graded roads after that.

The two vehicles proceeded in convoy into Cunnamulla, where they were going to have lunch before starting their journey. Apparently Monica thought that travelling with the gay couple was cooler than hanging out with her sister, so she sat in dignified silence in the Land Cruiser's back seat, while Robin joined Chloe in the back seat of the rental. Mike seemed to have no problems handling the vehicle during the short drive to town; in fact, it was all they could do to persuade him to take time out for lunch before starting the three-hour drive to Yowah.

Dave had chosen the town's restaurant as their lunch venue rather than one of the pubs, given the nature of the party, and that worked out well. The grub was simple in the best ways, and plentiful, and the conversation was promisingly cordial. Even Monica deigned to enjoy herself for a while.

"Can I hang with you guys?" she asked Dave and Nicholas afterwards.

Dave glanced at the other four who were still strolling down the pavement, chatting away. It seemed that Robin and Chloe were firm friends already; apparently they were bonding over a shared love of a series of films that Dave was only vaguely aware of. "If it's okay with your parents," he said to Monica, "it's okay with us."

"It's not, like, you have to talk to me or anything. I'll just listen to my music."

"That's fine," said Nicholas.

"And you don't have to watch what you say around me. I'm not a child."

"Understood. And if you did want to talk with us, that would be fine, too."

She went a bit pink, as if both pleased and embarrassed, so they let her turn away and slip her earbuds in.

Dave went over to the others, and rested a heavy hand on Robin's shoulder. "Can you put up with this one," he asked Mike and Suzanne, "if we stick with the current seating arrangements?"

Everyone was perfectly happy, so soon their small convoy was heading west along Adventure Way, with Dave in the lead. They stopped in Eulo for a cuppa and comfort break, and then continued on until they reached the intersection with the Opal By-Way which would take them to Yowah.

Once they'd made the turn, Dave pulled over to the side of the road, and switched off the Cruiser's ignition. Mike pulled in behind him neatly enough.

"Is something wrong?" Nicholas asked, though he didn't sound very worried.

"Nah," he replied, with a reassuring smile – though he flicked a glance in Monica's direction, trusting Nicholas to understand that meant Dave was being discreet. He climbed down from the cab, and went to say to the others, "Thought we could stretch our legs for a minute. How're ya goin', Mike? It's about another fifty clicks from here …"

Everyone was amenable to taking a short break. They all took a drink of water, and no one minded being reminded to wear their hats – not even Monica, thank heavens, who wore a straw hat with a wide circular rippling brim which Dave assumed she thought was cool.

That was all well and good – but his real reason for stopping was to check out the vehicle he was sure had been following them, more or less, since Cunnamulla. Soon it caught up to them, and passed without pausing, continuing along Adventure Way. It was a Land Rover Discovery, and Dave would have sworn the driver was Ted Walinski.

Dave had booked two of the cabins at the caravan park, one for each family. It had already been a long day, so they all concentrated on doggedly sorting out the luggage and settling in. A quick meal at the café brightened everyone up, though there were no disagreements about the notion of having an early night.

Soon after they'd all said goodnight, however, Dave heard a shriek and then further sounds of consternation from the neighbouring cabin. He headed over there at speed, with Nicholas and Robin at his heels. Dave wasn't overly surprised when he discovered the cause.

Monica was standing in the main room of the cabin with a green tree frog nestled trustingly in the palm of her hand. Her mother and sister, meanwhile – and even her father – were backed up just about as far away from her as they could get. "Are you kidding?" she was asking. "He's gorgeous! I mean, how *green* is that?" She lifted her hand, and Monica and the frog gazed intently into each other's eyes. "Aw … look at him … such a sweet little bloke."

Dave stood there just within the door, trying not to laugh, while Robin stayed by his side and peered at the frog from a safe distance.

Nicholas, of course, had no qualms about wildlife. "*Litoria caerulea*," he announced as he walked over to join Monica in her intent examination. "The Australian green tree frog. What a beautiful specimen! Where did you find him, Monica?"

"In the bathroom!" Suzanne announced with a horrified shudder. "Speaking of which … is it clear now?"

"Yes, Mum," replied the long-suffering Monica. "You're safe!"

"Oh, thank God," Suzanne muttered fervently – and made a dash for it round the edge of the room, keeping as far away from Monica as she could.

"How do you know it's a bloke?" Nicholas was asking meanwhile, leaning in close and gently prodding a finger at the frog as if wanting to turn it over and examine its chassis.

"Nicholas!" Dave protested.

Nicholas straightened up and looked at him. "Ah. Of course. I always forget that rule. Don't discuss the genitalia of frogs in front of the clients."

Monica snorted, Chloe giggled, and Mike did a little of both – while Robin dropped his face into his hands as if even he was occasionally befuddled by his beloved uncle.

"Come on, Monica," said Dave, thinking he'd better restore order. "I'll show you what's to be done with your new friend." He tilted his head towards the door, then led the way out.

She followed him trustingly enough, but protested, "You're not going to hurt him, are you?"

"Absolutely not."

Nicholas was walking with Monica, while the others hung back near the cabin, still keeping a safe distance. "A wise man once told me," Nicholas confided to Monica, "that people respect life out here."

The dark night hid Dave's smile.

"It's a beautiful country, but it can be harsh, so we all help each other out."

"Even the frogs?" Monica asked.

"Even the frogs," Nicholas affirmed.

A moment later Dave stopped by the large bucket kept near the amenities block. The sulphuric smell of the artesian bore water was stronger there, but Monica didn't seem to mind, and the frog certainly didn't. "Monica, if you pop him in here, he'll be taken out to the big dam in the morning, where he'll go on to live a long and happy life."

"Are you having me on?" she asked, hanging back.

"No." Dave shook his head solemnly, then indicated the bucket. "Look, he already has a mate to keep him company."

Monica edged close enough to peer in and see the other frog sitting there. "Won't they get bored? What are they going to do all night, sitting in a bucket?"

Nicholas's mouth quirked wickedly, and he was just about to answer – before Dave's look cut him off. "What?" Nicholas asked with a show of innocence. "I was only going to say they'll sing to each other, and maybe perform a duet or two."

"Sing?"

"Yes, that's their mates we can hear now," Nicholas whirled a finger through the night air.

Monica tilted her head to listen properly. "Oh! I thought that must be some kind of weird bird."

"It's the frogs. They'll be going all night, I'm afraid," said Nicholas. "But they sound happy, don't they?"

"Yeah …" she reluctantly agreed.

"Your friend will be fine – and he'll be happier still once he's at the dam tomorrow. Anyway, even I'd rather sit in a bucket outside on a night like this, than be stuck in a bathroom."

"True," she said, stroking the frog's back with the tip of her finger. Finally she drew near, and gently placed the frog in the bucket beside his mate. "Goodnight," she wished him. "Sweet dreams – and sweeter songs."

Then they all trailed back towards the cabins.

"Uncle Nicholas …" said Robin. "You'll check our bathroom, won't you? Very carefully."

"Of course," was the brisk reply. "Monica and I will be on regular Frog Patrol, I promise. Won't we, Monica?"

"Too right," she agreed with a laugh.

And finally they all started to settle, humans, frogs and all.

Dave loved the cool quiet peace of an Outback dawn. He woke early the next day and wandered down to the edge of the tiny town, to gaze across the fossicking fields and the wide flat land beyond. The enormous sky arched above in all its magnificent clarity. Everything was hushed for those last few minutes as the eastern sky shaded from blue to rose to gold. Then the sun lifted into view, and already the air felt a little warmer, and the frogs started singing along with the cicadas. Somewhere behind him, a screen-door swung smartly shut. Dave smiled, and headed back to the caravan park.

Robin was the next one to emerge from the cabins. He wandered towards Dave, who was taking care of the Cruiser. "Morning, Robin," Dave said. "Sleep all right?"

"Yes, thanks. How about you, Uncle David? Did you miss sleeping on top of the car?"

"Car?" he asked in horrified tones. "What car?"

Robin rolled his eyes. "The Land Cruiser. Did you miss her last night?"

Dave had to smile, but he said, "We only do that at the waterhole, you know."

"Uh huh, sure. Well, you know, what you do in the privacy of your own garage is none of my concern ..."

A chortle burst out of him. Maybe Robin wasn't quite the innocent they'd assumed.

"We're all aware that Nicholas has to share your affections with ... What have you named her?"

"Mate, it's just the Cruiser."

"Uh huh. Dave and the Cruiser, sitting in a tree, K I double S I N G."

He shook his head. He had no comeback for that. "I got nothin'," he admitted – though he was saved a moment later by Monica walking past in a set of black pyjamas, with another green tree frog in her cupped hands. "Morning, Monica."

"Hey," she greeted them, with a lift of her chin, and stayed her course towards the amenities block.

Dave trailed after her just in case, to make sure that nothing dire had accidentally happened to the other frogs – but there were three of them now in the bucket, and they all seemed perfectly content. Monica crouched down to place the fourth one in there, too. "They really will be okay, right?" she asked.

"Absolutely. The bloke and his wife who run this place, they'll come by soon – on Frog Patrol," he added, remembering Nicholas's term for it. "One of them will clear the bathrooms before people start using them, and they'll do the run out to the dam ... Actually, if you want to get dressed, we could go with him. Or we could offer to do the run ourselves, and we'll be back in time for breakfast."

Her eyes lit up. "Cool!" She was already on her way back to their cabin. "I'll have a quick shower, all right? Don't let them go without us!"

Dave laughed, and returned to where Robin was propped against the Cruiser, contentedly checking his phone, then chuckling as he thumbed in a message or a Tweet. Well, at least Dave had one happy client, and it seemed he had a happy young family member as well.

After breakfast, the seven of them did the opal tour, which involved visiting an underground mine as well as a working open-cut mine. In both, they were shown the layers of sandstone and clay – and in between the two, the shallow layer in which the Yowah nuts might be found.

The guide was full of advice for their own fossicking ventures, so they were all keen to pick up the fossicking licences that Dave had already organised. Then he had to exert a bit of authority to insist everyone had a quick lunch before they drove down into the fossicking fields.

Mike, Robin and Chloe decided to find a couple of spots in which they could dig, while Suzanne, Monica and Nicholas wanted to 'noodle' or wander around looking for bits of 'colour'. Dave knew from past experience that it was surprising how much could be found on the ground, or in the mullock heaps. White fellas had been mining at Yowah since 1883, but until recently most people had only been interested in the precious opals to be found inside Yowah nuts. The 'matrix' stones, where specks and veins of opal graced the red-brown ironstone, had been discarded – but were now very popular. Dave found them just as beautiful as and even more intriguing than the proper opals, if he was honest.

There was no shade at the fossicking grounds, and the sunlight reflected back off the exposed clay and sandstone, occasionally creating a really harsh glare. Despite the fact that Nicholas was wearing his Akubra and sunnies, Dave wasn't surprised when Nicholas came over to quietly say he was going to head back to the cabin for a rest. "I just want to cool down," he explained apologetically.

"Not a problem. I'll drive you back."

"There's no need. It's not that far; I can walk."

"I'll drive you back." Dave jogged over to let the others know he'd be back in a few, and then walked with Nicholas over to the Cruiser. Five minutes later, even Dave was glad to be in the leafy shade of the caravan park, so he could imagine how relieved Nicholas was.

"Thank you, David. I'll be fine from here. Don't worry, all right?"

"Of course I worry," he said mildly. "That's my job." They exchanged a quick kiss before Nicholas climbed out of the Cruiser. "I put your lime juice in the fridge," Dave continued, "and there's plenty of bottled water in there, too."

Nicholas turned to smile at him with affection. "I love you," he said, before closing the passenger door.

"Love you, too," Dave replied, knowing Nicholas could lip-read at least that much perfectly well.

The affection warmed, and then Nicholas turned away to walk slowly yet steadily towards the cabin.

Dave turned the Cruiser and headed back to take care of his other charges.

The next day, though still warm, was a little cooler and a little cloudier, so Nicholas was comfortable enough to stay with the others through a long morning of fossicking. As it drew near lunchtime, however, he did take a sieve and a bucket of dirt and rock over to the slice of shade thrown by the Cruiser, and sat there on the ground to patiently sort through it all looking for colour.

Chloe and Mike each found a small Yowah nut that morning, which created a great deal of pent-up excitement, as of course they wouldn't know what was inside until the nuts were broken open. Nicholas observed in a learned manner, "For now, the opal inside both exists and *doesn't* exist ..."

Which made Suzanne and Robin crack up with laughter, while Monica hid an amused smile, and murmured, "Schrödinger's opal."

Dave, Mike and Chloe exchanged baffled looks.

Meanwhile, Suzanne had happily accumulated a small collection of chips of matrix opal found while noodling, to which Monica had been discreetly adding. "They're not worth anything, I know," Suzanne said, "but they'll look very pretty in a little bottle of water on my windowsill, and I'll shake them up so it looks different every day."

"Like a snow globe, only with opal!" Chloe agreed. "And they'll sparkle in the sunshine!"

In any case, Dave thought he could safely add Suzanne to the 'satisfied client' list.

After lunch at the café in the community centre, Dave took them all to his mate Ned's shop where – after the tension increased unbearably throughout his quiet examination – the two Yowah nuts were sliced neatly in half down their longest dimension. Of course, there was nothing of value to be found within. Chloe seemed the most disappointed, as her nut contained a core of solid powdery clay, which was the usual result.

"Chances are only one in a thousand that you'll find an opal inside," Ned told her, in commiserating tones.

"And how many have you cut lately?" Mike asked.

Ned's smile glinted in the shadow of his beard. "Reckon I'd be in the nine-hundreds."

"Well, then," Mike concluded, "we might get lucky later in the week."

Mike's was empty but at least in an interesting way: the hollow inside formed an almost perfect sphere. With a slice taken off the curve underneath, and a bit of surface buffing, each half could sit like a small bowl.

"What are you going to put in there, though?" Monica asked. "They're tiny! No use at all."

"I shall buy a pair of opal cufflinks," Mike replied, on his dignity, "and keep one in each half." And he headed off to browse the items that Ned had on display.

The others all followed him, and from there they descended into groans of yearning and adoration and despair. Dave was the only one to hang back, knowing how it went … The items on display and for sale were beautiful – probably far beyond anything they'd imagined. But the most gorgeous specimens were also expensive, and rare, and therefore out of reach of most – though Dave saw that Mike began keeping an eye on what Suzanne was drawn to, so perhaps he could afford to really indulge her. For those without his deep pockets, the display both provoked their determination to do some serious fossicking, and also made them realise how unrealistic their hopes were of finding anything significant. All of which was why Dave tended to let people have a good fossick for a while before confronting them with the reality.

As the others wandered off to do some more browsing in other shops, Dave stayed behind to thank Ned, who hadn't charged them for cutting open the Yowah nuts. "No worries," was the reply. Then Ned lifted his chin in a westerly direction. "Beauty of a sunset this evening, I reckon."

"Thanks," said Dave, nodding an acknowledgement. At least sunsets were freely available to all who cared for them.

The sunsets at Yowah were generally known for their magnificence. Dave wasn't sure if there was a reason for that, or if it was just one of those things, but he made sure to never miss an opportunity to enjoy one.

That evening as the sun was westering, he and the Cruiser led Mike and the rental out to the Bluff, an abrupt cliff face a few clicks east of town. They were in plenty of time, so they drove to the further edge, where there was a view out across a seemingly infinite plain containing nothing but mulga. Around the lookout area were tall cairns made of piled stones, none of them fixed by anything other than judicious choices. They – except for Monica, who seemed to have reverted to being too cool – marvelled at these and at the view for a while, before heading back to the western edge of the Bluff, to look out over the town of Yowah to the far horizon.

For a while the sun hid behind a thick band of cloud – but then at the last possible moment, the light broke through, and the vista turned from gold to red to purple above them, lit by the sun and shaped by the clouds, as beautiful as any opal. They were all gobsmacked – even Monica.

It lasted for several minutes, in a hush that felt eternal, until eventually it began to fade, and then the sun slipped below the edge of the Earth, and the sky became a deepening purple.

They all remained quiet and still, except that Dave turned to Nicholas where he sat perched beside him on the Cruiser's roo bar. Dave turned to Nicholas, as gorgeous as any sunset, and took his face in both hands and kissed him, a real full-blooded kiss. When they broke apart, Nicholas grinned at him, lopsided with joy as if he hardly knew whether to laugh or weep – and then the two of them belatedly realised that everyone else was watching, but all of them fondly.

Nicholas announced, "Don't get me wrong, I love a good sunset, but David is by far the most beautiful thing in my life."

Dave found that he was a bit pink-cheeked at the compliment, but otherwise he was perfectly fine and bold and happy. It finally dawned on him that he hadn't felt embarrassed or self-conscious about loving another man for *ages* now. Which seemed like good cause to kiss Nicholas again, so he did, dragging him close with both arms wrapped around his waist – and the others cheered or laughed as was their wont.

They returned to the caravan park during the long dusk, and to everyone's surprise found Charlie sitting outside the cabins, tending a wood-burning barbecue with potatoes already baking in the embers.

"Charlie!" Dave was pleased enough to give the man a hug. While they were close he took the chance to quietly ask, "Anything wrong?"

"Nothing urgent." Charlie drew back to look him in the eye. "Nothing that can't wait."

Dave nodded, tried to wrestle his curiosity into submission, and turned to beckon the Baldry family forward from where they'd paused at a tactful distance. "Let me introduce you to a good mate of mine …"

Charlie announced that barbecuing was blokes' business, and delegated the work accordingly. Robin was sent to fetch folding chairs for the three women, and once they were settled comfortably he was to take care of their drinks and any other requirements. Dave and Nicholas were to chop vegetables and get them marinating in olive oil and lemon juice. Meanwhile Mike and Charlie took care of the sausages and steak – and then, in the last few minutes, they chargrilled the veg. Nicholas and Dave cut a cross into each potato, and pushed in a knob of butter and cracked pepper.

The results were plentiful, fresh and tasty. "I think I've died and gone to Heaven!" declared Suzanne as she finally sat back, replete.

"Awesome …" Chloe managed faintly.

"I'm taking you along on all my trips now," Dave said to Charlie.

"Like you could afford me," Charlie scoffed, which made everyone laugh while hanging onto their full bellies.

Charlie had put a large billy of water on to boil for bush tea, with a few gum leaves in it for flavour. Once that was ready, they all sat in comfortable silence for a while with the steam from their mugs of tea rising to the stars. The frogs sang to each other, while the cicadas provided a percussion track.

Eventually Robin said, "Charlie …"

"Yeah, mate?"

"Can you tell us a Dreamtime story about opals?"

Charlie rumbled in thought for a long moment before saying, "Reckon I can."

"Oh! Thank you."

Another long moment passed before Charlie began, but everyone was suitably patient and expectant. "There are different stories about opals in the different regions of Australia," Charlie said, "and I got to thinking that is probably right, because the opals are different, too.

"The story about opals in this country starts with an Ancestor in the form of a pelican. Old man pelican would travel and travel a long ways, from country to country and further. He'd carry his own food and drink in his dillybag: the pouch beneath his beak would always be full of water and fresh fish.

"One day, though, he died, on a hill north of here."

Robin asked in a hushed voice, "How did he die, Charlie?"

"Reckon I can't tell you that bit of the story."

"That's all right. I didn't know that Ancestors could die, though. I thought they just went back to sleep."

Charlie tilted his head in consideration. "Some do, some don't. You're right, though; most are sleeping." Then he continued, "When old man pelican died, the water in his pouch flowed out and made Cooper Creek – and the Barcoo River," Charlie added, with a nod to Dave – "and filled them full of fish. And it was his blood, seeping into the earth, that made the gold and the opal."

"Cool …"

"Some while after, the people living south of here, maybe in what we call New South Wales now, they wanted to know what was up here. So they sent another pelican to explore, and to tell them what he'd learned when he returned. He carried his water and his fish in his dillybag, because it was a long journey, and he'd been told not to stop.

"Pelican became tired, though, and he flew down to rest on top of a hill. This was the same hill where the Ancestor had died, and when Pelican looked about, he was filled with wonder at all the beautiful colours in the ground. No one had ever seen opal before, so he was very curious, and he started tapping at the stone with his beak. Soon he was chipping away at it, and sparks were flying, pretty in the sunlight. But the dry grasses nearby caught fire, and the flames rose high, and then they spread … The fire spread all the way back to Pelican's people where they were camped. That was the first time those people used fire for cooking their meat, just as we've done tonight. And that fire came from the opals, and the opals came from the blood of the pelican Ancestor."

"Oh!" cried Suzanne, who'd been absolutely spellbound – she burst into applause, before guiltily looking around to see if that was improper or not.

But of course it was fine, and everyone had already joined in, while Nicholas expressed thanks for them all.

There was a comfortable lull while people contemplated the story and what it might mean, and then began thinking about what might happen next. The evening wasn't quite over yet.

"Okay," said Monica, her tone indicating a determination to be brave. She stood up, then stilled again – when one of her hands started marking time, Dave realised she'd been listening for a rhythm from the frogs and cicadas. Monica looked at Chloe, nodding with the beat now, and Chloe picked it up with handclaps and a shift of her shoulders. They'd obviously done this many times before, though their parents were watching in startled wonder. "Y'all ready for this?" Monica asked – and she started rapping.

"We're off on a trip with a bloke named Dave
Still waters run deep, he's a bit of a rave.
Nick is his man till death do us part,
They got two bodies, one soul, they got one heart.

"Robin's their guy, but he is his own man,
He loves Tony and Pepper, he's a bit of a fan.
And God made Charlie from the rock and the clay,
Skin dark as night, and eyes bright as day.

"So we're off on a trip through this wide brown land,
And thanks due to Dave, we got it all to hand.
We got frogs, we got opals, we got purple skies,
And when we got baked potatoes, we don't need no fries.

"Yo," she concluded, and struck a pose.

The whole party – and half the occupants of the caravan park who'd gathered round – burst into delighted laughter and hearty applause. It was only now that Monica remembered to be embarrassed. She dropped her face into her hands with a groan. But Suzanne went to wrap her up in a great warm hug, and told her how magnificent she was – and the applause continued, while Robin declared, "That was wicked!" and Charlie agreed, "It was deadly, all right. The deadliest!"

"Nicholas," Monica said once things had quietened down a bit, "I'm sorry about 'Nick', but I'm not good enough to cope with three syllables."

"No need to apologise at all," he stoutly replied. "Nick is my rap name, don't you know."

It had been a really great evening, one of the best, but Dave was still relieved to finally get the chance to talk with Charlie. They sat at the kitchen table while Nicholas made a last round of tea, and Robin pottered about for a bit before saying goodnight and heading for his bedroom.

"So, did you have some news?" Dave eventually asked.

"Nothing urgent, mate, or I wouldn't have made you wait. Just talk about a mine meaning they'd put the railway through, and what that's gonna bring."

"People are still thinking about the jobs, then."

"Yeah. Can't really blame them."

"I know. But there are other things to think about, too."

Nicholas brought the tea over and sat down. "Cunnamulla is already on a railway line, isn't it?" he asked.

"It's the last stop on the line," Dave explained, "so they'd be extending it further west."

"Which means landowners along the way will be looking for recompense."

"And the two on the far side of the waterhole will be keen on a quicker way of getting their cattle to market." Dave sighed. "It'd mean massive infrastructure costs, though, even if they don't take it out as far as the floodplains."

"Mining's always high investment, isn't it?" Charlie observed with a shrug. "And if they reckon they're looking at natural ore, it's gonna pay its way."

"Yeah …"

Charlie left a long pause while they all gloomily contemplated the possibilities, tried to weigh the probabilities. Then he said, "You'll come with me to the reserve again, before you head home?"

"Yeah, I guess," said Dave, knowing he sounded reluctant.

Charlie cocked a curious brow at him, and Nicholas's expression was all sympathetic worry or maybe worried sympathy or whatever.

Dave confessed, "I'm just … letting them down, you know?"

"What, cos you're not black?"

"Well, yeah, basically. The Native Title thing was just a daydream, wasn't it? I was such an idiot to even –" Dave cut himself off, and changed track. "Thursday and his mob might be able to get the reserve extended. Nicholas and Lisa might be able to protect the butterflies and the wattle. Where does that leave me? There's nothing I can do, and that place, that beautiful place –"

"You sing the songs, mate. You tell the stories."

Dave stared at Charlie for a long moment, but eventually he had to ask. "And that's enough, is it?"

"It's the only thing," said Charlie. "It's what really matters."

Nicholas nodded. "That's right at the heart of it."

"That place would have died already, without you."

"I'm not – I'm not –" He almost groaned with frustration. "I'm not doing more harm than good?"

"No, mate," said Charlie. "Old man grunter chose you for a reason."

Nicholas took Dave's hand in his, and said, "None of us could have even *found* the waterhole without you."

"You're a good man, Davey."

"Hear, hear," Nicholas agreed, squeezing Dave's hand and smiling at him, Nicholas's lips curled with such exquisite fondness and his eyes shining with such affection that Dave couldn't fail to be moved.

"We've got one heart," Nicholas murmured late that night in the darkness of their bedroom, his palm pressed just to the left of Dave's sternum.

"Mmm …" Dave contentedly agreed. "I like that we've got two bodies, though." And he proceeded to demonstrate why.

On their last full day in Yowah, Dave and Nicholas got up just as the eastern sky was lightening, and walked down to the fossicking fields. They were already more than familiar with the area in which Robin and Chloe had been diligently working; it was straightforward enough to tuck a couple of uncut

Yowah nuts into the pile of dirt and rock they had yet to sort through, and a fragment of matrix opal as well. Then they headed towards the area where Suzanne had been noodling the previous day, amiably arguing as they did so about which direction she might head in next.

As they turned a corner round an outcrop of stone, they were startled to find that Monica had beaten them to it. She was crouched on the ground with her back to them, gently trailing a few fragments of matrix opal through the powdery dirt, before gathering them up again and scattering them in a long arc off to her right. When she stood and dusted off her hands, she looked around – and almost jumped out of her skin to see them looming behind her. "What are you two doing here?"

"Same as you, from the look of things," Nicholas replied with a grin. "That's good of you."

She shrugged. "You, too, then."

Dave said, "I guess we'd be overdoing it, if we left something here for your mum as well."

"You've taken care of the kids already?" Monica asked – and when they nodded, she pondered for a moment. "Well, we might be making it really obvious if everyone gets lucky this morning, but I'll show you where Dad was working, if you like. We'd better look out for him, as well!"

They were soon done, and then the three of them started back up the track towards town. In the still air they could hear the humans, pets and wildlife all starting to wake up. The day had already lost the dawn chill. "Going to be a warm one," Dave remarked. "You might want to take it easy today, Nicholas."

Dave received a small wry smile in reply, equal parts gratitude and stubbornness with a dash of sorrow.

"Well, before you put your feet up, Nicky GT," said Monica, "we're on Frog Patrol, remember? Otherwise half the tour group will be unfit for anything at all."

"Nicky GT … ?" Dave echoed.

"All I need now is some serious bling," Nicholas said in tones of complete satisfaction. "Oh, and a hit record, of course."

Monica snorted.

Suzanne soon started finding her seeded colour, and criss-crossed that area bent almost double in order to closely examine the ground.

Chloe was next – finding not one but both Yowah nuts. Her joy quickly faded, though, when she caught Robin looking indulgent, and realised she'd been fooled. Then suddenly she powered up again. "Robin! Did you put these here for me to find?"

He quickly shook his head. "Not me." Robin glanced at Mike, though, obviously thinking him the mastermind.

"It wasn't us, either," Mike said.

Chloe thought for a moment, and turned to Dave with a quizzical brow.

"My services don't extend that far," he announced with a straight face.

"Don't look at me," Nicholas added. "It's enough being on Frog Patrol every minute of the day."

Mike concluded, "You're becoming a very successful prospector, Chloe!"

"Yeah, you really are," Robin agreed, obviously believing in their denials.

Chloe's face as she basked in Robin's compliment was like a flower at last unfurling in the sun.

When she finally returned to her fossicking, Dave saw that Robin's expression fell into dismay.

The week drew to a close all too soon, and the two families prepared to part at Cunnamulla airport. Mike shook Dave's hand in a particularly emphatic way, and said a few un-blokey things about what a truly wonderful time they'd all had. "Thank you," he continued. "You made everything easy, and I don't doubt we did more in a day than we'd have managed in a week without you. It's been an absolute pleasure."

"No worries at all," Dave replied. "And I really appreciate you letting me bring Nicholas and Robin along. We've had a great time, too."

"It's been wonderful having them with us – and meeting Charlie, as well. We couldn't have asked for more."

Not everyone was as happy, of course. Chloe was in tears at being parted from Robin, and Robin was dealing with that with all the awkwardness of youth. The two of them were already following each other on Twitter, and had exchanged email addresses, but at Chloe's age every parting was tragic and forever. Meanwhile, Monica had withdrawn into her cool shell again, though she did make sure she caught Nicholas's and then Dave's eye, and nodded an acknowledgement. Dave knew she'd enjoyed the trip, perhaps almost despite herself – and it was Monica who finally put a comforting arm around Chloe's shoulders, and led her off towards the plane.

Mike and Suzanne both thanked Dave and Nicholas again, and farewelled Robin, and then they left, too. Dave and Nicholas watched for a while longer, to make sure everything was shipshape, and then they all three waved as the plane taxied off to the runway. Soon it lifted into the air, banked to the east, and was gone into the haze. The living quiet of the Outback returned.

Dave had his arm around Nicholas's shoulders, and Nicholas had an arm likewise around Dave's waist. Nicholas leaned in closer for a moment, tucking his head in against Dave's. "It's been the most perfect week," Nicholas said. "I've loved every minute of it."

"Me, too," said Dave, tightening his hold for a moment.

"Thank you, David," Nicholas said, standing tall again so they could talk eye to eye.

"No worries, mate. But what for?"

"For this." Nicholas gestured broadly. "For us, for our life here. For everything."

Dave looked at this man, his husband, and said, "I wouldn't have it any other way."

seven

Dave, Nicholas and Robin met Charlie at the Aboriginal reserve the next day. As before, Dave and Charlie went to sit with the gathered Elders while the other two went to hang out with the more sociable group in the shade thrown by the store and the neighbouring trees. Dave sat near a vacant spot, but a little removed from the circle, and Charlie settled beside him. Whatever certainty Dave had found last time he was here had gone again. He felt humbled. Thursday nodded a genial greeting at him, but Dave managed little more than a glum grimace, and then lowered his head.

After a while, Thursday prompted, "You think you bring bad news, Dave."

"Yeah. I should have known. Well, I did know, but I forgot for a while. It's hard to be taken seriously, when I'm obviously not Indigenous."

"You got no business with that place!" one of the others declared. "Charlie got no proper business, neither."

Dave had lifted his head at that, instinctively firing up, but he took a moment to consider his response. "The place itself, the waterhole, that's what's important. That's what comes first."

"You got no business performing the ceremonies."

"If there's someone more … suitable to pass the songs to –" Dave felt a stab of pain even at the thought – "I'll pass them on."

"No," said Charlie in his stubbornest tones.

"If there's someone from your people who'll take it on," Dave insisted – but then he stalled.

"No," Charlie said again. "It was the Ancestors put these thoughts in my head. That old man grunter chose you for that place."

"And who'll come after me?" Dave asked, honestly wanting to know. "Who will I pass the songs to when it's time?"

Charlie shrugged that off. "It's not time yet."

"Well, anyway," Dave said, turning again to Thursday. "I don't think I can help much in using the white man's law to protect the site. Nicholas is doing what he can for the butterflies, and his friend for the wattle. We think they're unique, and they're going to have them officially listed as 'Vulnerable'. That might be enough in itself."

Thursday nodded thoughtfully.

"But," Dave continued, "I'm going to have to ask you to try to extend the reserve, to include the waterhole in your care. Will you do that, do you think?"

Another nod from Thursday, but the man who'd protested Dave's right to perform the ceremonies shifted ominously.

"I'm not asking for my own sake," Dave insisted, "but for the land's."

"We can apply to have it gazetted," one of the women said, "if you can tell us where exactly the waterhole is. None of us mob have been there."

"Fair point. I've been thinking about that. I've been thinking we probably need to hire a surveyor of our own. Even if that means we're opening it all up." Dave grimaced. "So, anyway, if you can … I think the sooner the better, right? Once people hear a mining company's involved, God only knows what interests come into play."

She nodded, and they all settled back into their thoughts, though some of them were happier than others.

After a while, when it felt as if it were about time to leave, Dave said a general "Thank you", and stood up.

"I'll stay here, mate," Charlie said, looking up at him.

"You sure? You want us to wait?"

"Nah, you go on. Young Robin'll be wanting his dinner. I'll get a lift into town later with one of this mob."

Dave went to round up his family, and take them back into Cunnamulla.

They'd decided on an early start the next day, so as to get back to Brisbane in reasonable time. Dave took their overnight bags out to the Cruiser while the morning was still cool and quiet and full of possibilities. Nicholas and Robin had gone to breakfast already, and promised to have a coffee ready for him when he met them there. All was well. Dave had slept soundly, and was recovering his usual sense of optimism. But a chill took him as he headed round to the back of the Cruiser and stowed the bags securely. Something was wrong.

Once he'd closed the rear door, he paced pensively along the length of her, carefully checking her out. The Cruiser was dusty, but that was only to be expected at this point. Her tyres seemed fully inflated. There weren't any scratches he didn't already know about.

It was only when Dave reached the bonnet and looked across that he realised. There was a bull's-eye break in the windscreen, with a starburst of cracks radiating out. He stood and stared at it for a long moment. It was serious; it would have to be fixed before they left Cunnamulla. But how the hell had it happened?

There was no way he wouldn't have noticed it the previous evening; it hadn't happened while he was driving from the reserve into town. Which meant that overnight, some kind of accident – or a deliberate drunken prank … Not that there was a guilty rock sitting on the bonnet or on the road nearby … Dave frowned, and pulled out his mobile.

First he took a few photos of the damage from different angles. Then he called the local garage, and asked if he could bring the Cruiser in for a replacement windscreen. They agreed, and said they could get it done pretty much right away.

By the time Dave had driven the Cruiser down there and walked back to the hotel, his coffee was cold.

"Did you report it to the police?" was Nicholas's first question once the coffee was replaced and Dave had explained where he'd been.

"No. Didn't seem much point."

"But –"

"It's fully covered by insurance. It's just annoying, really. We'll be leaving an hour later than we'd planned, but that's about all."

Nicholas let a beat go by, before saying, "Someone has deliberately damaged the Cruiser, and you're letting them get away with it?"

Dave shrugged, though of course it wasn't that he didn't care. "There's no proof it was anything but an accident. What could the police do? For that matter, there's no proof it didn't happen on the road yesterday."

Nicholas glanced from Dave to Robin and back again. "But it didn't, did it? We'd have known, wouldn't we?"

Dave brought out his phone, and showed Nicholas the photos.

"We'd have definitely known," Nicholas concluded. "So there's three witnesses, anyway."

"Three witnesses to say it didn't happen while I was driving – but that's all."

They pondered this. Dave drank his coffee.

Then Robin had a bright idea. "What about CCTV? There'll be footage of whoever did it. Or whatever happened."

Dave found himself reluctantly smiling. "Not out here, mate." He added with mock severity, "*Don't* run wild."

Nicholas was looking troubled, and absently rubbed a hand against his forehead in the way that always made Dave a bit anxious. That was the worst part about this: it pained Nicholas. Not that Nicholas was concerned for himself. "The poor Cruiser," he murmured, reaching to gently squeeze Dave's shoulder.

"Don't worry," said Robin. "Uncle David will kiss her better. She'll be *fine.*"

"Eat your breakfast," Dave advised with a mock growl.

Of course, every time they drove through a town or some other location that had mobile reception, Robin's phone chimed to announce incoming messages. One, which arrived while they were passing through Dalby, seemed to put Robin in pensive frame of mind. Dave kept an eye on him in the rear-view mirror. Robin was doing nothing more than staring out the window at the unchanging scenery, so after about fifteen minutes of that Dave said, "You right, mate?"

Nicholas stirred and looked around, having fallen into his own reverie. "Robin … ?"

"I'm all right." But Robin sighed, and after a moment he said, "Uncle Nicholas …"

"Yes?"

"Has it been … you know … a real pain for you? Me being in love with you, I mean."

"No," Nicholas warmly replied. "No, of course not." He shifted around in his seat, so they could talk more directly. "Why do you ask?"

Robin grimaced, and didn't say anything.

Dave glanced at him in the mirror, and guessed, "Text message from Chloe?"

Another sigh, before Robin admitted, "Yeah." Then he asked Nicholas, "What am I supposed to do? I mean, it's not like … it's not as if there's anything I *can* do! I'm *not* going to fall in love with her. She's just a kid, for a start!"

"Be kind to her," Nicholas promptly replied. "Be a friend. Be patient. That's a great deal to be getting on with. And it will pass. These things always do."

"Do they?" Robin asked in sceptical tones.

"Yes. You know – this is a secret, all right? But when I was her age … and when I was your age, too, for that matter! I was in love with someone who would never love me back. It could have been horrible, it could have broken my heart, but he was kind to me, and actually now I think it was the … second most perfect thing that ever happened to me."

Robin had his head down, but Dave sensed somehow that the mood had changed.

"If you can be her friend," Nicholas forged on, "Chloe might one day look back on this as something that made her happy."

Silence.

"Robin?" Nicholas prompted.

A muffled noise from Robin might have been a sob or a groan – but turned out to be a laugh. Robin was suddenly grinning at Nicholas and bubbling over with mirth. "I know you were in love with Frank Brambell, Nicholas!"

"Oh." Nicholas seemed rather affronted. "Do you?"

"And for that matter, you still are, a little bit. Sorry, Uncle David."

Dave laughed, too. "No worries," he assured Robin. "It was one of the first things I knew about your uncle. We'd hardly even said g'day and he told me he had a thing for chauffeurs."

"Were you driving at the time?"

"Yeah."

Robin thought that was hilarious. "Oh right, it's such a big secret he just blurts it out as soon as he sets foot in another country … Which is why I don't believe you, Nicholas, with all your 'This too shall pass'. As if it ever passed for you. And David still isn't totally over Denise either – are you?"

Dave cast him a wink via the mirror. "Yeah, maybe not."

Nicholas was still looking a bit pinched around the mouth. "How did you know?" he asked Robin when he could get a word in edgewise.

"Well … when I was young, I spent most of my life paying attention to you, didn't I? And there you were, spending most of your life paying attention to Frank."

"God! I tried so hard to be discreet. For his sake, you know? I never wanted to get him into trouble."

"It's all right," Robin said. "I don't think anyone else knew. Or didn't take it seriously, if they caught a hint. Except Simon, of course."

Nicholas shifted to sit back properly in his seat, as if he needed the support. "Simon knew?" He glanced at Dave –

And Dave confirmed this with a nod. "Simon knew."

"Oh God. Well. I suppose Simon always knew everything that was going on, didn't he?"

"Pretty much," Robin and Dave chorused – and then shared another laugh.

Poor Nicholas had just had his world rocked. But it didn't take him too long to rally. "All right, then. You have some good examples to follow, don't you, Robin? You treat Chloe as well as I treated you. As well as Denise treated David. Maybe not quite as well as Frank treated me," Nicholas added with a nostalgic kick to his smile. "You do that, and chances are she'll remember this last week as the happiest idyll of her life – at least until she meets the guy or girl who'll love her back." Nicholas's hand slipped over to rest warmly on Dave's thigh. "And then you'll have stood her in good stead, because her heart will still be whole, and her own to give."

Robin was gaping in wonder at all this. Eventually he blurted, "Nicholas? I do love you, you know."

Nicholas turned to smile at him with wistful whimsy. "I know, my dear. And I love you, too."

Despite which, Nicholas was soon back to bothering over Robin. "Did you hear him referring to Chloe as a kid?" he demanded of Dave once they were home, and closed bedroom doors separated them from Robin. "And Monica – who's two years younger than him – referred to him and Chloe as kids! I mean, that really was the most perfect week, don't get me wrong, but wouldn't you have expected him to befriend the older of the pair?"

"Aren't girls meant to grow up quicker than boys?" asked Dave. "At least, that's what I was always told. Maybe it was just cos Denise was always smarter than me, though."

Nicholas offered him a brief sympathetic smile, but was not diverted. "Monica was quite mature for her age, I suppose, and there's no denying Robin tends towards the opposite."

Dave emptied their bag of dirty clothes into the laundry hamper. "Maybe you could try taking him a little more seriously, Nicholas. Robin can seem like a different person when you're not around. When he's with you … it's almost like he reverts to the eleven-year-old boy you used to know back when you were living in England."

"Oh … I hadn't thought of that." Nicholas sat on the edge of the bed. "Oh yes, I see. I, uh … I know I get a bit giddy and drop at least a decade of intelligence when I'm with my father."

That made Dave laugh. "Giddy, yes. I reckon it's one of the reasons he adores you. But no one would ever call you unintelligent!"

Nicholas favoured Dave with a warm glowing smile – but then reverted to the topic of Robin with an irritable shrug. "Do you know, I'd almost started to think that the gap year was a good idea? I was beginning to think he wasn't ready yet – not for an intense course like PPE, anyway."

"Not that I know anything about the course, but I bet he's ready. He's clever, like you are – and I'm sure he knows his own mind, Nicholas."

But that led directly back to the question of Robin's sexuality, and it seemed Nicholas wasn't ready to talk sense about that yet.

There was a knock on the front door a couple of days later. Dave went to answer it, having no idea who it might be as they weren't expecting anyone. He opened the door to discover two men on the patio who didn't seem to be selling religion or a new energy plan. One of them was a white man with a sun-browned face, and the other Asian, perhaps Chinese – both of them middle-aged and wearing suits. "Can I help you?" Dave asked, having even less of an idea about what they wanted.

"Mr David Goring Taylor … ?" asked the white man.

"Yes."

"My name is Harvey. Fred Harvey. I represent the Reddy Eight mining company." He paused, and lifted a brow.

Dave's gut plummeted. "Oh. I see."

"Yes. I believe you've had some dealings already with a Mr Walinski, whose services have been retained by Reddy Eight." When he didn't receive a reply, Harvey indicated his companion, who stood a step beyond his right shoulder. "This is Mr Teng, who represents one of our major investors."

Teng respectfully inclined his head in greeting, so Dave did likewise – but he didn't make a move to open the screen-door, and he said in rather hard tones, "You come to my home … ?"

Harvey grimaced in what might pass as an apologetic expression. "If Taylor Outback Tours had a shopfront or office, I would have met you there. But it doesn't."

"And you couldn't have called first?"

"Would you have agreed to meet us?"

It was Dave's turn to grimace in acknowledgement. "Guess I might have put you off."

"But we need to talk," Harvey implacably continued. "Don't we?"

Dave weighed this up, but he concluded – as he supposed he must – that he should probably get this over with. "All right." He unlocked the screen-door, and swung it open. "Come in, then," he said ungraciously.

"Thank you," said Harvey. Teng offered another polite nod as he passed.

Dave didn't let them any further than the lounge room – which he and Nicholas used, though it was the most formal room of the house, such as it was. Of course Nicholas came through from the family room as soon as he realised they had guests, so Dave did the introductions. "This is my husband, Nicholas. Nicholas, this is Fred Harvey from the mining company, and Mr Teng from their investors."

"It's a pleasure to meet you," Nicholas smoothly replied, being the polite Englishman he still was – though Dave noted he didn't offer to shake hands with either man, nor did he offer their guests tea or coffee. "Would you care to sit down?"

Once they were all seated, each pair facing the other across the coffee table, Fred Harvey said, "I'll get right to the point, then."

"Please do," said Nicholas.

"I think we all know why Mr Teng and I are here. It seems, based on a very small sample, that there is a source of hematite out west of Cunnamulla. My company, Reddy Eight, naturally has an interest in that. But before this goes any further, we need to assess what's actually there." Harvey left a pause, but no one leapt in to either agree or disagree. "All right, then. It's not a difficult process to prove that enough volume of the stuff exists to make it worth our while to move in – or to prove that there *isn't* enough, if that's the case. I suspect it's in all our interests to at least establish that much."

Dave slowly took that in. Eventually he asked, "So, just to clarify, you don't even know for sure yet whether there's actually enough there to be worth mining?"

"That's correct, yes."

"And if there isn't … ?"

Harvey lifted his hands palm-out. "Your problem goes away."

Dave huffed a breath in surprise. "Okay, so what do you know about my 'problem', as you call it?"

Harvey took a moment with that, but then said, "We understand that there's some kind of … problem in accessing the site. That you're the only one who knows the way in." He shifted, betraying a moment's uncertainty. "To be honest, no one can explain to me exactly why that is."

Which drew another huff from Dave. "Not sure I can exactly explain that, either. But," he added, "that's not the whole story."

"No. There's a Dreamtime site out there, and songlines," Harvey said to Dave. Then he turned to Nicholas to add, "Not to mention vulnerable flora and fauna."

"Okay," said Dave. "So whether you understand or not, you've got to know I'll do anything I need to do to protect that place, and the things that live there."

"I respect that," said Harvey. "I do."

"Okay …" Dave repeated, knowing he sounded unconvinced.

"So why are you here?" Nicholas asked.

Harvey shifted forward a little, and said very directly to Dave, "We want to offer you a finder's fee, of sorts, if you'll lead Mr Walinski and a small team – geologists, surveyors – to the location of that hematite."

Dave stared back at him for a long moment, before glancing at Nicholas.

"Reddy Eight is in a position to be … generous. Very generous."

"I'm not the kind of bloke who can be bribed or bought," Dave said, though without much umbrage.

"I respect that as well," Harvey smoothly replied. "I'm discussing a service that you can provide us, and fair recompense for it."

"I've already got all I need," Dave said, with another glance at Nicholas.

"Though you probably already know that," he added with a bite to his tone. God only knew what kind of access a moneyed-up mining company had to individual financial records let alone more personal stuff.

"I understand, Mr Goring Taylor."

"And a lot of the locals are keen to have you out there. You don't need to deal with me to set that up."

"But it seems we need you to help find the place."

Dave ignored that for the moment. "And you'll need to be dealing with the Murri, because it's all going to end up as part of their reserve. If you're talking recompense, they're the ones who should have it."

"I admire your principles, Mr Goring Taylor. If you would prefer us to make a donation to the Aboriginal reserve rather than pay you a fee, that would be fine with us, and of course a certain percentage of jobs would be offered first to anyone in that community. Whatever you might think, Reddy Eight is not interested in destruction or desecration, but in cleanly extracting a resource that ultimately we all benefit from – and not only our friends in China," Harvey said with a nod to Teng. "Over half the weight of your Toyota Land Cruiser is due to the steel in it, you know."

Dave's reaction this time went beyond a huff; it was more like a bark of humourless laughter. "Now you're really getting personal!"

Harvey shrugged in something like an apology. "I only wanted to make a point, not cross any lines."

"All right." Dave took a long moment to consider, but he didn't figure anything had really changed. He looked at Nicholas again, but apparently Nicholas was trusting Dave to know what was right to say and do, just as Charlie was trusting Dave, and Thursday and his mob as well. Dave sighed. "Well," he finally said, "it's not that I'll never help, but I'm not ready to help yet. I need to make sure the Dreaming site will be safe. Once I'm sure of that, and I'm sure it's what most of the locals want, then I'll do whatever needs to be done. But not right now, and probably not real soon, either."

"Thank you, Mr Goring Taylor." Harvey stood, and offered his hand.

"Well, don't thank me yet," Dave said. But he also stood, and he shook the man's hand – and then Teng's as well.

"Thank you, sir," said Mr Teng, in an accent that mingled China and Australia.

"Right," said Dave. And he saw them to the door.

Once they were gone, Dave locked up again, and sank back against the door wondering what the hell would be thrown at him next. All he had to deal with immediately, however, was Nicholas stepping close, and lifting a gentle hand to cup Dave's face. "You were brilliant," Nicholas said.

"I wasn't. I'll try to be good enough, anyway."

"You're *bloody brilliant*," his husband insisted – and he pressed close for a full-on kiss as if that would prove it.

The next day that Nicholas went in to the uni, Dave drove Robin in to join Nicholas for lunch, and then the three of them went to talk with Lisa Munroe. Dave hadn't met her before, but could immediately see what had Robin interested. Anyone who had a taste for Nicholas could hardly fail to appreciate her tall lean figure and long face: the first impression of their likeness was almost uncanny. But she wore her dark hair in a thick plait, and her pointed chin was her prettiest feature while with Nicholas it was his plump pink lips. And Dave soon decided that while she had a lovely dimpled grin, it couldn't compete with Nicholas's range of smiles.

Robin was obviously still besotted – though, while he wasn't playing it cool, he seemed more thoughtful than starry-eyed now. Dave contemplated the situation while Lisa and Nicholas compared notes on their half-completed nomination forms for listing protected wildlife. Being bisexual himself made it easy enough for Dave to understand Robin being romantically inclined towards both genders. It was more difficult to get his head around the notion of not wanting to have sex with someone he was in love with – actually *not even wanting to* as opposed to not being able to for whatever reason. But Dave figured that if Robin was happy that way, there was no point in wanting him to be unhappy. What the odds were of Robin eventually meeting someone likewise inclined, and the two of them both falling in love … well, Dave didn't like to think. But surely it *was* possible. And in the meantime, there was … studying and working and eventually becoming prime minister, not to mention family and friends and all the other good things in life.

It must have seemed a bit weird for Lisa and Nicholas to finally look up from her computer and find both Robin and Dave in a reverie. Especially Dave, who was hardly known for being a thinker of any kind, let alone a deep one. Lisa laughed, and asked, "Solving the meaning of life, are we?"

Robin blushed – and Dave didn't have anything on his mind that he particularly wanted to share, so he glanced around in desperation, and as luck would have it the relevant paperwork was right there on Lisa's desk. "Just having a ponder on the Nature Conservation Act," he asserted, knowing that he probably wasn't fooling anyone.

There was more laughter in response, but then Lisa got right back to business. "I've been thinking about the waterhole itself," she said in serious tones. "Nicholas told me your theory, David, about the pool itself being fed directly from the water table."

"Um … yeah," Dave replied, wondering if he'd ever had a theory before. Obviously there was a first time for everything.

"If that's the case, then it raises the issue of any changes to the water table possibly affecting the level of water in the pool – and *that* might have a detrimental effect on the flora and fauna."

"Oh," said Dave, starting to scramble towards the full implications. Nicholas got there before him, and looked horrified. "You mean," Dave said, "even if the mining company kept their distance from the place itself, they might affect the water table, and that might …"

"Exactly."

"Oh God."

Nicholas stuttered a couple of times before managing to say, "The waterhole seems so timeless. Changeless. As if it hasn't been disturbed by anything for centuries."

"As if it's still dreaming," Dave found himself saying.

Nicholas stared at him, and then lifted a hand to his head as if he could hardly bear his own thoughts. "I've been thinking of it as almost … eternal. But nothing in nature is. Or only when you take the largest view of it all. The conservation of matter and energy means nothing is ever lost, but everything eventually changes. Everything has its season."

"A *natural* season," Robin protested. "Just because it will eventually be destroyed doesn't give us leave to destroy it now."

"Spoken like a true philosopher!" Nicholas replied, reaching a hand to ruffle Robin's hair. "And maybe you can tell me what there is in that field about a change in perception. I feel as if my perspective has just shifted one hundred and eighty degrees … One moment I'm thinking that the waterhole is changeless, and the next I'm thinking that the place exists in such a delicate balance, that actually it's … unbearably fragile. And that scares the dickens out of me."

"All right," said Dave. "So that's one more thing to take into account."

"David, we really need to push this whole thing as hard as we can."

"I know," he replied, though he still felt as if all the important stuff was out of his hands. "You guys keep working on your nomination forms. We'll take Lisa out there as soon as we can – and if either of you have any ideas about a surveyor we can take, someone to help us pin down the location, that would be great. Otherwise I'll be looking up the Yellow Pages."

Nicholas came to sit by Dave, looking troubled and impatient. He didn't say anything, but then he hardly needed to.

After a thoughtful pause, Robin said, "Uncle David … you know that man you talked to about Native Title? He'd know someone, wouldn't he? Or he'd know who to ask. I mean, they'd need to establish boundaries and such all the time."

Which earned Robin a broad happy grin from Lisa, and a particularly beautiful grin softened by affection from Nicholas – in the midst of which Dave's thanks went pretty much unheeded. Not that Dave minded one little bit.

The phone rang the next day, and Dave picked it up. "Hello, this is Dave."

"Hello, Mr Goring Taylor. This is Shirley Johns; I'm mayor of the shire council out at Cunnamulla."

"Ah," Dave responded rather intelligently, while reflecting that he probably should have been expecting this. "G'day, Shirley."

"G'day, David. Well, I won't beat about the bush, as you probably know why I'm calling."

"I can guess."

"Yes. I've had a couple of meetings with a Mr Fred Harvey of Reddy Eight. I believe you've met the man. He's interested in our natural resources, and we're interested in his investment. But we need your help."

"Yes, well, I'm interested in protecting something that's even more precious than iron ore."

"I'm sure I don't need to explain what a boon for the community it would be – and for the whole region – in terms of jobs and infrastructure. We'd be very grateful to you."

Dave sighed. "And I bet he passed on my answer. That hasn't changed."

"I confess I'm rather confused, David, about no one seeming to know where this place is. Can you at least tell me whose property it's on?"

"No, I can't – and that's not me being difficult. We've never been able to really pin it down."

"Mr Harvey mentioned that they've tried to locate it from the air as well. Apparently iron ore is quite obvious if you know what you're looking for. But they're left feeling as confused as I am."

"Well, I'm not surprised," Dave said – though he was, rather, by all of that. "The place isn't easy to find. I can't even explain why, really, unless you're prepared to believe that the Ancestors are protecting it, or something."

"I see," she said in sceptical tones.

"Shirley, once I'm sure the Dreaming site will be safe, I'll help. I've just got to be certain of that first. It's in *our* interests, now, to be able to locate it on a map, so I'm working out how to do that. But you'll understand I have my priorities."

After a moment she sighed, as if accepting at least a momentary defeat. "I understand – and for what it's worth, you were already well respected in town, David, just as your father always was. That's only increased in recent days."

He huffed a cynical laugh. "Flattery's not gonna do it for you, Shirley."

"It's not flattery if it's true. I'm sure I'm not speaking for myself alone when I say I very much appreciate the stand you're taking."

"Right. Okay, well, if that's the case, then if you can do anything to help Thursday's mob in extending the Aboriginal reserve to include the Dreaming site, I'd appreciate it. And I'll do what I can as soon as I can. That's as much as I'm able to promise right now."

"I understand," Shirley repeated, "and I'll do what I can as well, I promise you that. Thank you, David."

"Thank you, Shirley." And they each said goodbye, and hung up.

So there was someone else to add to the mix of interests precariously balanced around this issue. Dave's head hurt. But there was one thing he never lost sight of, and that was his sense of the true priorities. That had to count for something, surely.

There was another phone call late that night when the house was dark and they were all fast asleep. Nicholas kept a handset by his side of the bed, because of course a call in the middle of the night to him meant England. "Hello?" Nicholas answered blurrily, sounding as if he wasn't even half awake.

There was a long empty pause during which Dave stirred, and Nicholas turned on the bedside lamp.

"Hello?" Nicholas tried again, glancing at Dave with a frown. "Simon, is that you?"

Nothing.

"Father … ?"

Nothing. And then the line cut out. Dave could hear the dial tone kick in.

Nicholas turned off the handset and dropped it into his lap, before rubbing hard at his face for a moment. Then he picked up the phone again, and used speed dial to call the Goring family home in England. "Simon? It's Nicholas. Did you just try to phone us?"

"No, I didn't," Dave could hear Simon reply.

"We just had a call, that's all, but I missed answering it. I couldn't think who else it would be."

"If you can hold the line, Nicholas, I'll check with your father. Is everything all right with you?"

"Yes, everything's fine. I was calling to make sure everything's all right with you!"

"It must be very early in the morning there."

"Two-thirty," Nicholas replied, having checked his watch.

"No wonder you were worried." A few moments later, Richard had added his reassurances to Simon's that all was well.

"Never mind, then," Nicholas concluded. "Sorry to bother you. It must have been a wrong number."

"Goodnight, Nicholas," Richard said in farewell. "It was lovely to hear your voice. Sleep well now."

Nicholas put the handset back in its cradle, turned out the light, and lay back down in the bed. Dave shifted in close to snuggle up to him. "All right?"

asked Dave.

"Yes." Nicholas sounded wide awake. "There was someone on the line, you know. It wasn't just dead. I could hear them breathing."

Dave frowned, and finally suggested, "Some idiot dialled the wrong number, and then was too much of a wuss to admit it."

"I suppose," said Nicholas.

"Get some sleep," Dave urged. "Everyone's fine. It's okay to sleep now."

Nicholas sighed. "I suppose," he said again. But Dave suspected he'd be too fretful to really rest.

eight

Nicholas and Dave had decided that Dave would manage the next tour trip on his own. His clients this time were a bunch of blokes in their early twenties who basically wanted to camp out, go off-roading, do an extended crawl of Outback pubs, and generally behave like larrikins. Dave had figured it wouldn't be much fun for Nicholas and Robin to tag along, apart from which the clients might feel their style was being cramped.

Robin seemed to agree it would be a good idea to sit this one out; nevertheless he indulged in a bit of a sulk, perhaps because he'd enjoyed their Yowah trip so much. Nicholas likewise seemed torn in two about the decision, though in his more reasonable moments he agreed that he and Robin were better off at home. As for Dave, even after all these years he couldn't leave Nicholas behind without a serious pang.

This time he met up with his clients – six of them, almost indistinguishable from each other at first glance – in Toowoomba. From there a convoy of the Cruiser, a client's own Ford Territory, and a rental four-wheel drive headed through Dalby to Chinchilla, where they stopped for lunch at the RSL. Dave was intending a sober trip, for himself at least, to help ensure he could keep an eye on the others' safety, but he had to have a Cascade in honour of Chinchilla native Pete Murray – a ritual Dave and Denise used to observe religiously. He had a private chuckle, though, at the thought of telling this lot Pete's butterfly story, as he'd told Nicholas back in the days when they'd first met. It would take Pete telling it to provoke a suitable reaction in these blokes.

Dave received a call that evening from Denise, though it wasn't for the sake of sharing the Pete-love. She was instead passing on a message. "It's the Barton station," she said. "You were heading there on this trip, weren't you?"

"Yeah, for the off-roading."

"They've called to say they're restricting access to their land."

"Really?" he responded, feeling somewhat mystified. "I've never known them do that before. Did they say why?"

"No. It was Daryl who called, and he sounded a bit odd about it, like maybe he didn't agree himself. But what can he do? They're entitled."

"Of course they are. All right. I'll just reshuffle my plans a bit. These guys won't even notice."

"Having fun, are you?" Denise asked in wry tones.

"They make me feel old," Dave replied, "but mostly in a good way. Sometimes I even feel mature!"

"Crikey! Hang on to that, then."

"Will do."

It took a great deal of maturity for Dave not to swear loudly enough to wake the town early one morning in Charleville, when he came out of the hotel to find that not one but two of the Cruiser's tyres were flat. Luckily his clients were late risers, but by the time he'd swapped the wheels for the two spares, driven the Cruiser down to the garage and walked back, the blokes were straggling down for breakfast.

"We might have a slight delay in setting off," he announced. "I've had a couple of flat tyres."

"Oh," said Scott, the bloke who owned the Ford. "Is my Territory okay?"

"Didn't think to look." Dave accompanied Scott out to where the other two vehicles were parked, but they seemed all right, thank God or whichever Ancestor was watching over them.

"That's bad luck with the Cruiser," Scott observed as they stood there contemplating the Territory. "Both on the same side, I guess? You must have run over something that wouldn't say die."

"Bad luck, yeah," Dave agreed, provoked into further thought. He followed Scott back inside, and sat there frowning over a strong coffee. The thing was, Dave had never had more than one flat tyre at a time, and he certainly hadn't noticed anything wrong while driving the previous evening.

When he headed back to the garage, they announced they hadn't found any damage, though as requested they'd replaced the inner tubes anyway. "Better safe than stuffed," one of the mechanics opined. "Don't wanna get stuck out there."

"Ain't that the truth," Dave agreed. He contemplated the discarded inner tubes, which had been reinflated in an unsuccessful attempt to find the holes and patch them. "D'you think," he asked after long moments, "someone deliberately let them down? As a prank?"

The mechanic looked unimpressed. "Maybe. Can't think what else. Bit bloody-minded for a prank, but."

"Yeah …" Dave sighed, figuring he wasn't going to find an answer, or at least not that morning. "Look, would you keep them inflated for a while, and see if they do go down? It might be a really slow leak. Keep them, though. Sell them or use them, if they're okay. But I just want to know, one way or the other."

"No wuckers," the mechanic said, which of course was Australian for 'No fucking worries'. He lifted his chin in acknowledgement, and added, "Be seein' ya, then." The latter expressed a wish that it be so, and therefore that Dave stay safe out there.

"No wuckers," Dave replied.

Dave and his clients had planned to camp out that night. Of course Dave was an old hand at this by now, so he got the bulk of things set up efficiently despite the other blokes being more interested in teasing each other about who was going to share a tent with whom. Dave had his own tent, as usual, which was sacrosanct, and he managed to tactfully ignore the ribbing between his clients, who were obviously all concerned about being straight or at least being seen to be so. Some things were slow to change. Still, Dave reflected, they knew well enough that he had a husband at home, so they couldn't have been completely homophobic. "You all better sort it out," he eventually commented, "or one of you might end up sleeping in *my* tent."

There was a collective melodramatically indrawn breath, and then a solution was quickly found. Dave would be sleeping alone, which of course suited him perfectly.

It would be an understatement to say he was less happy with what he found once he'd further unpacked the Cruiser. A couple of items he took out were suspiciously wet – with water, thank God, rather than petrol or anything else – and when he finally got into the stuff stashed securely up against the back seat, he found that one of the containers of water was leaking. Maybe half of it was gone. Not that that mattered much in itself – Dave quickly checked the water they'd stored in each of the three vehicles, but the rest was all safe, and of course he always took as much water as he could reasonably carry on a trip. In this case, the seven of them could probably survive for a couple of weeks on what they still had, and they were actually planning to be back in town the next night.

However. Despite the fact that Dave always planned for accidents and emergencies – or maybe because of that fact – it was very rare that anything actually went wrong. And this loss of water followed hard on the heels of the flat tyres, and he'd had that broken windscreen not so long ago as well.

Dave upended the leaky container in order to save what he could, and they used the remaining water that evening. Nevertheless, once he'd had a ponder while cleaning out the Cruiser, Dave definitely felt he owed his clients an apology. "Flat tyres. Losing some of our water. I want you to know that I don't take these things lightly."

"No worries," said Scott. "It's clear you've got it covered."

Another one – named Matt – said, "Everyone told us how you haven't lost a client yet. Or not for years, anyway."

"Ha," said Dave, and reached to touch one of the larger branches which was waiting by the campfire.

"Anyone can have a run of bad luck," one of the others reassured him. Owen.

"Thanks. Well. I have a Plan B, C, D and E for just about everything, so I'm sure we'll be okay."

"Absolutely," they all agreed.

Dave sighed. Bad luck, Owen had called it. But Dave was honestly beginning to wonder …

The next morning, when they stopped just off the road for a tea break, Scott quietly approached Dave. Scott and his Ford Territory had been bringing up the rear in their convoy of three, and now he announced that he'd noticed something. "Maybe I'm just imagining things, but I think there's somebody following us."

"Why d'you think that?"

"Most of the time, there's just dust in the mirrors. But every now and then there's a tiny shape in the distance that looks like a four-wheel drive, and a dust cloud behind it."

"And that's just been this morning?"

Scott shrugged uncomfortably. "Dunno. Maybe yesterday, too."

Dave carefully didn't look around, but he asked Scott, "Can you see it now?"

"Nah … But you know … I don't have that good an imagination, yeah?"

"Understood." Dave thought about this while he drank about half a cup of tea. Then he said, "All right, if you don't mind helping, let's see if we can't sort out what's going on."

"Sure," said Scott.

So, next time there was cover enough to make it work, Dave pulled the Cruiser over and parked in the shelter of some trees and scrub. The other two vehicles carried steadily on as if nothing had happened, their dust clouds obscuring the fact that the convoy had lost a member.

Dave climbed out and watched the other vehicles for long moments, not really liking to let his clients head off on their own. Then he turned to peer through the foliage to see what, if anything, might be following them.

Soon enough, a pale-coloured four-wheel drive hove into view. Dave adjusted his glasses on his nose, and squinted hard. As the details came into view, Dave wasn't overly surprised to find that the vehicle was a sand-coloured Land Rover Discovery. Ted Walinski. And as far as Dave could make out, it seemed he was alone, or at least there was no one in the passenger seat, and no other vehicles following.

Dave took a breath – and just as the Land Rover pulled past the trees, Dave stepped into view with his hand out to flag the man down.

Walinski had obviously been fooled, but anyone driving out here needed quick reactions; he hit the brakes, but let the Land Rover continue on a little, stopping at an angle a wary distance away so he could keep an eye on Dave and the surrounds as he slowly climbed out and down to the ground. "Mr Goring Taylor," the man said, while pausing nearer his own vehicle than Dave's.

"What are you doing out here?" Dave asked in unimpressed tones.

Walinski shrugged. "Guess you know the answer to that."

"Following me."

Another shrug, which was neither confirmation nor denial.

"I'll save you the trouble. I'm not going anywhere near the waterhole, not this trip."

"Well, maybe you are, maybe you aren't."

Dave crossed his arms, and favoured the man with a hard gaze. "One of my water containers sprang a leak yesterday. Do I have you to thank for that?"

Walinski looked genuinely shocked. "No! Hell no."

"And two flat tyres, back in Charleville. Know anything about that?"

"No – and I wouldn't –"

Dave sighed, and lifted a hand to indicate it didn't need to be said. "No, all right, I know that." After all, Dave was talking about life-threatening stuff, and anyone who really belonged out here would never stoop so low.

Walinski gestured towards the Cruiser. "Everything all right?"

"Yeah," Dave replied with a sigh. "I was just wanting to ambush you."

"Looks like the cavalry are coming, anyway."

Dave shook his head in bemusement to see – and hear – the two vehicles containing his clients returning at speed. "I didn't ask them to do that. They were meant to stay right out of it." The young blokes were hollering as if they thought Dave might need rescuing. "Here," said Dave, holding his right hand out to Walinski. "So they don't get the wrong idea."

The two of them shook hands very deliberately, making a bit of a show of it, so Dave's clients were relatively calm again by the time they stepped out of the vehicles. "All right, Dave?" asked Scott.

"Yeah, mate, I'm fine."

Walinski backed away a little, but asked, "D'you need water? You said you'd lost some."

"No, we're fine. There's plenty left. Thanks, though."

"All right." Walinski lifted a hand in a general farewell, and headed back towards his Land Rover. "See ya, then."

The others called, "See ya!"

But Dave followed after Walinski, and said to him quietly, "Look, I told you and I told Fred Harvey: I'll help as soon as I can. I've just got to make sure that place is safe first. Then I'm not gonna stand in anyone's way."

"Understood," said Walinski. And they shook hands once more and then parted.

Denise called the next day with news of someone else who'd withdrawn off-road access to their property.

"For everyone," Dave asked, "or just for me?"

"Well, for everyone. I guess. I don't know … No, surely for everyone!"

"Right." Still. Dave had to wonder if he were being completely paranoid, thinking there was a message in there for Dave alone.

"Man, that was a bit of a rough trip," Dave announced, pretty much as soon as he was safely back home in Brisbane.

"Missed me, did you?" Nicholas asked cheekily.

"Yeah, o' course. But to be honest I was glad you and Robin didn't come." Dave groaned a little as he stretched out his shoulders and tried to roll the kinks out of them. "Have to admit I'm pretty knackered."

"Here, then," said Nicholas, "I have the solution." He came over to where Dave was propped against the breakfast bar, and pressed a mug of steaming hot tea into Dave's hands, pressed a kiss to his temple.

Dave grinned at him, still a total sucker for this guy, and happily so. "That'll do it, every time."

Nicholas gave him another kiss for that. "Was it worse than you've already told me?"

"Well, no … But you know that I like things to go smoothly."

"Ah, but what's the point of having backup plans for your backup plans if you don't use them every now and then?"

Dave grimaced a quibble, though he had to acknowledge the point.

"And I'm sure your clients were more than satisfied. In fact, if I know you, they were downright happy about the whole trip!"

"Well, yeah, I did try to keep the drama off their radar."

"They probably didn't think it was anything more than business as usual, and I know very well you would have kept them safe."

Dave took a couple of mouthfuls of the tea, and then put down the mug so he could instead drag Nicholas close and wrap both arms around his waist. "Trying to talk me out of a good worry, are you?"

Nicholas rested his hands on Dave's shoulders and considered him for a long moment – and then he sighed and sagged a little, though he kept enough distance from Dave that they could talk to each other directly without squinting. "You haven't used the S word, but I know what you're thinking."

"I need to apologise for something … ?"

That drew a muted laugh. "Not *sorry*, David. Sabotage."

Dave stared at Nicholas, his gut sinking. Stupidly, it made the problem all the more real to finally be voiced. And by Nicholas, too. So much for Dave protecting his husband from the nastier side of life.

"That's what you're thinking, isn't it? The windscreen, the tyres, the water. The landowners withdrawing permission for you to go off-road."

"Yes," Dave at last said a bit hoarsely. "That's what I'm thinking."

"But you don't think that … Ted Walinski, for instance, is part of it."

"No, I don't think he is. Not that he's not trying in his own way … Well, he doesn't worry me, not anymore. And maybe the rest isn't really a planned thing, but random. A few different people getting it into their heads to play pranks. Not like a planned campaign, you know?"

Nicholas's hands tightened on Dave's shoulders. "But it could become dangerous. What if you were out there in the middle of nowhere, and someone let all the Cruiser's tyres down?"

"I'd use the pump to refill them."

"And if you couldn't? I mean, what if the inner tubes were damaged?"

"I'd phone Charlie, and ask him to come get me."

"What if –"

"I'd grab the map, the compass, as much water as I could carry, and walk to the nearest station or town. And I'd leave messages every way I could, to let you all know where you could find me."

A silent moment passed, and then Nicholas reluctantly smiled. "I know you have all the answers."

Dave returned the smile, which prompted Nicholas's to become a more genuine thing. "So you don't need to worry about me, right?"

"Not so much about you, no. Although of course I do. As your husband, that's my privilege."

They shared a soppy grin, before Dave prompted, "What else are you worried about, then?"

Nicholas sighed, and pulled away from Dave's embrace. He paced off past the dining table, and then came back again. "What I'm worried about is the waterhole and the butterflies."

"I know," Dave said, making himself sound far more reassuring than he felt. "I know. I'm doing everything I can, Nicholas, I promise –"

"I know you are."

"The trouble is, I know I can't do anything much myself – but with you and Lisa, and Thursday and his lot, I figure we'll make it happen. We'll put it beyond any question of harm."

"But that's the problem," Nicholas replied in deadly calm tones. "It can never be put beyond any question, can it? It can never be entirely protected."

Dave stared at him, and his thoughts took on a desperate tinge. He tried to say something, but his throat was dry, and anyway Nicholas forged on.

"The waterhole exists in such a fragile balance. It wouldn't take much to destroy the habitat, or change it enough so that the butterflies can't adapt. If there are people out there willing to commit sabotage, then it has to occur to them that … that they could simply make the environmental problems go away. If there's nothing left to protect –"

"But, then, what's the answer?" Dave blurted out. "If we just leave the place be, how long d'you think it will remain hidden?"

"I don't know."

"Sometimes I think someone's gonna spot it one day – from the air, maybe, or some random off-roader is gonna crest that ridge. Other times, I think … that place is elsewhere … it's elsewhen. And no one's ever gonna find it. Especially not if I don't risk leading anyone there or leaving a trail to follow."

Despite being a scientist, Nicholas was obviously intensely interested in this notion. "I don't pretend to understand – it's an entirely different way of thinking – but you're saying the waterhole is caught in its own Dreaming."

"Maybe. I just don't know. I wish I did. And anyway, what about the songs … ?" Dave slumped a bit, and went to sit on the nearest dining chair. "I still need to – Well, no … maybe I need to let that go. Let the whole thing go. It's not like many people agree with what Charlie did, passing the songs to me."

Nicholas dropped to his knees before Dave, and grabbed onto him hard. "No. No, you mustn't give up on that. It's important. Whoever's causing trouble, they can't make the cultural problems go away, can they?"

He grimaced again. "It's not like there's a whole lot of people who take me seriously."

"But it's still a Dreamtime site."

"But only if … if the relationship between the land and the people is still alive. And I don't count."

"If the reserve is extended to include the waterhole, that makes it clear enough, and then the Murri will be better able to help protect it."

Dave sighed, and said in a small voice, "I'll just need to find someone – the right someone – to pass the songs to, and –"

"No, don't do that," Nicholas said, shaking him gently. "Not until you really have to. Old man grunter chose you, remember?" He laughed a little under his breath, but continued with quiet sincerity. "I realise you don't believe in the stories and songs in a *literal* way … but there's some part of you that … I don't know. That *feels* them as true. If that makes any kind of sense."

Dave stared at the man in mute wonder.

"Or, um … a part of you that *knows* the necessity. That's probably better. You can sense there's a reason for all this, a good reason – and seeing as it's about us humans being an intrinsic part of the environment, rather than something separate from it, then actually I think it's a bloody excellent reason!"

"Oh," said Dave.

"On top of which," Nicholas said, sailing remorselessly on, "it does you good. It makes you happy. After you've been singing the songs, you look so … utterly peaceful. It's lovely to see. I love being there with you afterwards. You're just so very … *you*."

"Oh," he managed.

"I don't want to give that up for *my* sake, let alone yours," Nicholas added with a laugh. He was about to sit back on his heels, having made his point, but Dave grabbed onto him in turn and leaned his head in close.

"It's the second best thing in my life," he admitted in a mumble that only Nicholas would understand.

Nicholas guffawed. "Second best after the Cruiser, I assume."

"Idiot," said Dave. And they shared a grin, and Nicholas's love and happiness shone bold from his bright eyes – and in that moment Dave felt as if he could take on the whole world and the horse it rode in on as well.

nine

What Dave found frustrating, though, was that there still seemed to be little he could do. He asked Charlie to come to Brisbane for a few days so Dave could talk through the idea of actually lodging a Native Title claim. "It probably wouldn't come to anything, but at least it makes the point."

"Nnn," Charlie replied rather noncommittally.

"That guy I talked to," Dave persisted, "Martin Bandjara. He said he wanted to test the idea, or he'd like to, anyway. And for that they need someone to give it a try, I guess."

"Mmm," said Charlie.

Dave lapsed into silence, having been round and round the matter a number of times, and feeling further than ever from a resolution.

The four of them were lazing about on the back patio while the banana palms rustled soothingly. Charlie had a beer, but the others were on water-and-lime. Robin was curled up on the swing chair with Nicholas, though he didn't look quite as blissful about it as he'd used to.

Nicholas was also fretting over something. Dave watched him patiently, until at last Nicholas stirred himself to ask, "Could I be part of the claim as well? Would that help or hinder, do you think?"

Which was rather unexpected. Charlie didn't react, even with an incoherent murmur. Dave scrunched up his face, and tentatively asked, "Because of the butterflies … ?"

"Well, yes. No. Sort of."

Dave glanced at Charlie again, but he seemed to have zoned out. Or was maybe mulling things over. "Sort of?" Dave prompted.

"I've just been thinking about the story. You know, the Dreamtime story about the waterhole. And I figured … I figured that it's *my* Ancestor who fell from the sky, right?"

No one responded, though Dave was listening hard.

"You know, I flew here, I came by plane … David, you came to meet me, I fell at your feet, and we … Well." Nicholas fell quiet, too.

Dave wondered what to say. But when he realised that Charlie was considering Nicholas thoughtfully, Dave decided to stay quiet at least for now.

After a long while, Charlie said, "You and Davey belong together, mate. You don't need no Dreaming story to tell you that."

"No, but … it kind of works, doesn't it? He even … I mean, if Dave's Ancestor is the Barcoo grunter, then he even made the butterflies that brought me back to him."

"It's a nice thought, mate," said Charlie.

"Are you saying … I can't be part of it?"

"You *are* part of it," Dave insisted.

"I don't think Native Title can be the answer," Charlie finally concluded. "It won't work, whether it's me or Dave or the three of us making the claim. We'd be putting a whole lot of time, effort and money into something that was doomed."

"Oh," said Dave and Nicholas, both sounding rather dejected. "That's rather … pragmatic of you," Nicholas added.

Charlie shrugged an agreement. A silence stretched.

After a while, Nicholas detached himself from Robin and came over to where Dave was stretched out on a recliner. Dave shifted up onto his side so that Nicholas could settle in behind him, spooning him closely in a comforting hug. Dave closed his eyes, and sank away for a while. This … *this* was home and hearth and all good things.

"So, Robin …" Charlie said. "I guess you'll be heading back to England soon."

"Three weeks and five days," Robin replied. "Granddad's coming here for the last ten days, and then we're flying back together."

"It'll be good to see him, that's for sure. Are you looking forward to being home again?"

"I suppose …"

Dave opened his eyes, though he didn't shift from Nicholas's warm embrace. He asked with careful neutrality, "Are you still thinking about staying here, Robin?"

Charlie chortled appreciatively. "You looking to emigrate, too, mate?"

"I was thinking about … maybe taking a gap year," Robin replied.

Nicholas had remained quiet and still through all this.

Dave suggested, "It only needs a slight adjustment in your ambitions. Prime Minister of Australia ain't such a bad thing to be."

Robin sniffed. "No … once I've served my terms in Britain … *three* terms,

I think … I might consent to become Governor-General of Australia instead."

Dave and Charlie both had a hearty laugh over this, and Dave asked, "Don't you think we'll be a republic by then?"

"I don't know …" Robin mused. "What do you think, Charlie?"

"I think we're a pretty independent mob," said Charlie.

"That's true," said Dave.

Nicholas shifted up onto an elbow, as if finally re-engaged by the conversation.

"But there's something to be said for the long-term view," Charlie continued. "I was reading the other day about how the British monarchy has been around for a thousand years. It's one of our longest surviving institutions. That has to mean something."

"Does it?" asked Dave, perhaps almost as astonished as the two Englishmen about where this was going.

"If they were doing such a bad job, they never would have survived this long."

"Right …" Dave prompted.

"And the current lot, they're a good mob. So, I figured, what we should do, if we want to be a bit more independent, but not throw out all the good stuff … What we should do is invite Prince Harry to be King of Australia."

Everyone stared at the man, absolutely stunned.

Eventually Nicholas said, "I like the way you think, Charlie. Very lateral!"

Dave let out a laugh, and said, "Yeah, Harry's enough of a larrikin!"

"What's a larrikin?" asked Robin.

"Oh, it means he'd fit right in." And by the time Dave had explained, Charlie had three firm converts to his rather unexpected cause.

Dave had a call from another of the landowners out west of Cunnamulla. By his reckoning he'd heard from all of them now. "Hello, Sandy," Dave said a bit guardedly once the guy had announced himself.

"Heh," said old Sandy under his breath, before launching right into the nub of the matter. "Now, I know some people have been a bit, uh … uncooperative lately. Not letting you drive off-road and such."

"Well," said Dave. "It's their right. I respect that."

"I know you do. I know you do. So I figured I'd just come right out and say it. We could do with the railroad coming out our way, mate. You get that, I'm sure."

"I do get that," Dave agreed. "Cheap and easy transportation. I understand."

"So you'll understand we have an interest in Reddy Eight finding this iron ore, then."

Dave gusted a sigh. "Mate, I'm not against it myself. I just need to make sure this place is protected. This particular place. It's … unique."

"Yeah, your bloke found his butterflies there."

"Yeah." *The butterflies he named after me*, Dave couldn't quite add. "They're unique, too."

"Hasn't he, like … brought some out and raised them? Like in that aviary up at Kuranda, maybe?"

"He tried a couple of times, years ago now, but it never worked. They didn't survive. And he says it's too tropical up at Kuranda, for a start."

"I'm not saying we shouldn't protect them in the wild," Sandy said all too reasonably, "but don't you think he'd better try again?"

"Yeah. Probably." Dave frowned over that, and wondered why Nicholas hadn't persisted. If they had Charlie or Thursday take care of the butterflies somewhere out there near Cunnamulla, where the climate wasn't all that different …

"Just in case," said Sandy.

"But that's not all, anyway," Dave insisted. He sighed again, and thought twice, but then forced himself to say, "I don't believe in much, mate, but this place – it's sacred. I gotta put that first."

"Yeah, and I get that. I do. I figure …" Sandy paused for a moment, before rushing on. "There's kind of a 'no man's land' out there, isn't there? Somewhere east of Henri Wilson's place, south of the Abo reserve."

"Aboriginal," Dave corrected him.

"I mean it fondly, and I say it to their faces."

"Even so."

"Right, well. South of the Aboriginal reserve, east of Henri's. That kind of area. Am I right?"

Dave tilted his head in a quibble that of course the man wouldn't see. "Close enough."

"It's all right, I'm not gonna do anything about it. Just wanted to be sure I was on the right page."

"Yeah, you are."

"Not that 'page' is the right word. That's kinda vast."

"Look, Sandy, just give me some time, all right? I'm sure you'll get your railway in the end."

"Right, mate. Well, if you or your bloke need anything, let me or the missus know."

"Will do," said Dave. And they said goodbye and hung up.

A moment later – Dave had hardly even turned away from the phone – it rang again. "Yeah," said Dave as he picked it up. "D'you forget something, Sandy?"

There was no response.

But the line wasn't dead, either. There was an uncanny sense of presence. An echo of a breath.

"This is Dave Taylor. Who's that?"

Nothing.

"Right. Hanging up now." He waited a moment, but when there was no response Dave cut off the call and returned the handset. After a moment in which the phone didn't ring again, Dave wandered into the lounge room to find Nicholas tapping away on his laptop.

Nicholas glanced up at him, and then looked again, apparently picking up on Dave's pensive mood. "Are you all right, David?"

"Yeah. Just more pressure. God, it's honestly not that I don't empathise … And then another wrong number. Getting a few of them lately."

Nicholas sat back and crossed his arms over his chest and stared at him. "To be honest, I was trying not to think about this. But they're not wrong numbers, are they?"

It took a moment for Dave to click. "Seriously? You think it's harassment? Along with the … sabotage?"

"I didn't tell you, but when you were away for that week, I got a call almost every single night."

"What!" Dave was furious – at whoever the idiots were, but also a little bit at Nicholas. "You should have said."

"I was going to that first night you were back, but then they didn't call again – or not in the wee hours, anyway – and you already had enough on your mind."

"Even so," Dave argued.

Nicholas frowned for a long moment, and then lifted a hand to rub at his forehead. "You know, I think my decision-making has gone a bit pear-shaped lately. Maybe I just haven't been getting enough sleep."

Dave swore under his breath that he could quite cheerfully kill whoever it was who'd been disturbing Nicholas. But at least this gave Dave one thing he could actually do something about. "Right. We're reporting it to Telstra. We can do that much, anyway!"

"No, you're right," said Nicholas, "and of course that's fine by me." His long fingers skittered across the keyboard as he closed whatever he was doing and opened a browser. "Come on, then. We can look up what to do on their website."

The three of them were eating dinner at the table in the family room that evening, with the ABC TV news on in the background providing its quiet litany of gloom, when a story came on about the Reddy Eight mining company. Dave reached for the remote to turn up the volume, and Nicholas glanced a plea to Robin to be quiet for a moment.

"Elvis Reddy, son of Noel Reddy and majority shareholder of new player Reddy Eight, had a surprise encounter today with business rival Leonard Harville," the newsreader said. The story cut to footage of a pair of men in business suits confronting each other with the puffed-up chests and sneering mouths Dave was more used to seeing outside pubs than courtrooms. Dave watched in disbelief as the scuffle became a swirl of colleagues, onlookers and reporters. The younger Reddy was soon yelling, and pointing hard accusations at the somewhat older and cooler Harville. "Just you beeping well wait," was the general tone of it. "I'm onto something beeping *big*." – Harville adjusted his cuffs. "Sure you are." – "Oh, you are going *down* ..." The story cut back to the studio. "Stock prices for both companies have remained strong," the newsreader commented, absolutely deadpan, "though Reddy Eight has edged ahead slightly this afternoon."

Dave just gaped for a while as the next story played, until finally he blurted, "*That's* what this is all about?"

Nicholas shrugged a little, though he looked uncomfortable. "What can you expect, really?"

"Dunno," said Dave. "The Quiet Achiever, maybe?" He got up and went to look for Fred Harvey's business card.

"What are you doing?"

"Dunno," he repeated. "Being outraged, I guess." Dave dialled the man's mobile number.

The call was picked up right away. "Harvey here."

"Dave Goring Taylor," he announced.

"Mr Goring Taylor. What can I do for you?" There was an edge in Harvey's voice indicating that actually he could guess.

"*That's* who you work for?" Dave demanded. "*That* tosser?"

"Well. He certainly helps pay the bills."

"And that's all that matters to you, is it?"

"No," said Harvey, with no heat or resentment.

"Did his dad just *give* him the company to see what kind of mess junior would make?"

"No," Harvey repeated in exactly the same tones. "That's really not how any of the Reddy family do business."

Dave took a breath, and found himself lifting a hand to clutch at his forehead just as Nicholas would when trying to cope. "Look. I'm trying to protect this sacred place, these unique butterflies – and this guy you're working for, all it means to him is a chance to score a point in a dick-waving contest."

After a pause, Harvey suggested, "A healthy sense of business competition –"

"Right."

"They're business men, Mr Goring Taylor. They keep score with dollars. Not inches."

Dave sighed. "Well, I guess I knew it was all about money, didn't I?"

"Not just for Mr Reddy," Harvey argued. "It's still money and jobs and infrastructure for the people of Cunnamulla, the Murri, and that whole area."

"Yeah, I know. And it's steel for my next new Land Cruiser."

"Yes, sir." Harvey left a pause. "Does this really change anything, Mr Goring Taylor?"

"No," Dave had to admit. "No, I guess it doesn't." He was just about to wind up the call, feeling entirely pathetic, when Harvey asked a question of his own.

"Mr Goring Taylor –"

"For heaven's sake, just call me Dave."

"Thank you. Dave. Have you seen the forecast for the coming rains? It's going to be one hell of a Wet season."

"Right …"

"Is the waterhole near the floodplains?"

Dave huffed a bit, and asked weakly, "Are you trying to trick me into revealing the location?"

"No, sir. I'm just passing on a concern."

"Well. I'll look into that, then."

"Right," they each concluded, before saying goodbye and hanging up.

Dave went back to the table and sat down by Nicholas. Robin had finished his dinner and wandered off somewhere, probably to his room, so Dave just launched right into the topic forever preying on his and Nicholas's minds. "Fred Harvey just said we should look at the forecast for this year's Wet. D'you know about that already?"

Nicholas was reaching for his laptop even as he replied with a frown, "No. Well, I'd heard it was going to be somewhat wetter than usual, but … are you saying he was trying to warn us about something?"

"Sounded like."

"God … All this time we've been fretting about anthropogenic threats, and it may all come down to a natural hazard instead."

Well, that was a new word for Dave, but he got the general gist. Within moments they were looking at a map of the Channel Country, the vast area through which the Georgina River, the Diamantina River and Cooper Creek drained into Lake Eyre. "Kati Thanda," Nicholas corrected Dave, giving the lake its proper Indigenous name.

"Kati Thanda," he agreed. "But the waterhole's hundreds of clicks away from all this, isn't it? A long way south-east of Channel Country."

"Yes …" Nicholas agreed slowly, his fingertips tracing out the waterhole's likely location. They'd at least managed to narrow down the area which contained it. "If it was going to be affected, we'd have weeks of notice. These things don't happen quickly."

"But what would we do in those weeks?"

Nicholas cast him an uneasy glance. "I'm not sure …"

Dave persisted. "What about the water table, and the pool at the waterhole? Would a heavy Wet affect that?"

"Possibly. Though the water in the pool has remained level no matter what the season when we've visited, so I'm hoping that –"

"But if it floods," Dave persisted. "If it reaches high enough to affect the wattle and the butterflies."

Nicholas blanched, though his long fingers were as nimble as ever, darting about the keyboard and calling up information about the weather forecasts and likely effects. "If it floods, then it would have happened before at regular intervals. Perhaps every hundred years or so; that kind of timescale."

Dave was trying to understand so hard that his head was hurting. "Does that mean the butterflies have survived other floods, though? If there even have been any. Or does it mean the butterflies have only been there since the last flood? In which case they'd be threatened by another one."

Nicholas glanced at him, full of misgivings.

"But, no – they're in the songs, aren't they? So they date back as far as the songs do, which could be thousands of years … Though I suppose the butterflies could have been added to the songs when they first appeared at the waterhole … Oh God, I just don't know."

"I don't know, either."

"I've been thinking," Dave continued, "we really should try to create a backup, you know? Transplant some of the wattle, and try to establish the butterflies elsewhere. Maybe there's a sheltered waterhole somewhere on the Aboriginal reserve that they'd let us use."

Nicholas had sat back now, and was watching Dave carefully, with his hands resting cupped in his lap.

"We could fence it off, and there'd be someone there who'd help us take care of them. I know you haven't had much luck in bringing the butterfly eggs and such back here, but the climate wouldn't be so different out there, would it?"

There was a small but very genuine smile on Nicholas's face by now, and his eyes were glowing with affection. Once Dave had finally wound his way to a halt, Nicholas paused for a beat, and then leaned in and quietly teased, "You and your backup plans."

"Is it a good idea, though?"

"Yes. Yes, of course. And if we succeed with one colony, then we should try for more as well. I wonder if I could find someone out there who actually has an aviary ..."

"I'll ask Charlie to ask around."

Nicholas's smile had widened, but also turned poignant. "You know ... I'm so used to thinking of the waterhole as ... well, as *ours*. And the butterflies, too. I almost ... I almost didn't want to bring any of the butterflies back here. But we're going to have to share them, aren't we?"

"Yes," Dave solemnly replied, "I think we are. But we've had them to ourselves for years and years, haven't we?"

"So many good memories there ... The first time we made love. The first time we kissed properly."

Dave felt his cheeks heating, and other parts of him, too. "I know." He added with a wry grin, "It's not like we have to share *that*."

But Nicholas wasn't ready to laugh about it. "Lazing about, getting to know each other ... All those long conversations we had, all those words and thoughts meandering along the riverbeds, diverting into billabongs, flowing out into lakes ..."

Dave snorted a chuckle. "That must have been you. My conversational skills are more like a dry old creek bed."

"They are not! And anyway, we found other ways to communicate ... other things to learn about each other."

"Oh, is that what we're calling it now?" Dave retorted, his chuckle becoming a laugh.

Nicholas sighed. "I wish we could go out there again, just you and me alone for one last time."

"I know. But we really need to get a surveyor out there, and Lisa said she's gonna come, too, didn't she? And her partner."

"I suppose ..."

"And I don't know that I want to give Ted Walinski yet another chance to track us there. We should try to keep control over when and how this happens. Shouldn't we?"

"Yes – but can't we skive off 'real life' for a few days? Don't we deserve that? We could just drop everything and go tomorrow."

Dave frowned, not sure exactly how seriously to take Nicholas. This might be just a verbal whimsy of his, after all. "What about Robin? You're not suggesting we, uh … I dunno, leave him behind with Denise and Vittorio or whatever?"

While it was fairly obvious from Nicholas's defeated expression that he agreed they couldn't abandon Robin even to the care of their best friends, unfortunately Nicholas didn't voice a denial.

"Uncle Nicholas … ?" Robin was standing in the doorway, frozen in the act of bringing a used mug back to the kitchen.

"Oh God," Nicholas groaned – though he sounded more annoyed than apologetic. "I'm sorry, Robin, of course we won't go without you."

"It's all right," Robin replied, stiffly on his dignity. "I know where your priorities lie."

"Well, it's not as if we're going, anyway, so don't worry about it."

"Nicholas …" Dave murmured, wondering at this unusual ungraciousness.

"I'd understand," Robin said. "You can dump me at Denise's, if you want."

Nicholas shifted around on his chair to confront Robin a little more directly. "How can you possibly understand? You're asexual, remember?"

Robin flushed, and came further into the room, clutching at the mug. "I know about *love*, remember? I'm just not into sex."

That dragged a growl out of Nicholas. He sounded almost *agonisingly* frustrated. "I might agree that you know about love, if you didn't always fall for the inaccessible. Me. Lisa. That's not love, it's infatuation."

"Oh right," Robin scoffed. "So it was infatuation you felt for Frank, was it?"

Nicholas sniffed. "Ah, but Frank wasn't so inaccessible as all that."

"Nicholas!" Dave protested, knowing that if Nicholas were thinking clearly he'd be a lot more discreet.

A guilty look glanced off Dave, and then Nicholas continued a little more reasonably, "One day, Robin, someone you care for will be ready, willing and able to return the compliment … and you should at least *try*."

"Sure! And one day, Nicholas, you should *try* with a woman."

The two of them glared daggers at each other.

Dave sighed, and sat back in his chair. "That's enough from both of you," he said.

And maybe they even agreed, for the silence resounded. But Nicholas did nothing more than cross his arms, and Robin just lifted his nose and looked haughty.

"Look," Dave continued. "I have no idea what either of you can say to make this better, so I reckon you're just gonna have to agree to disagree. All right?"

Nothing.

"Isn't that what unconditional love is all about? Not, uh … imposing conditions on each other," Dave finished rather weakly.

Robin stared hard at Nicholas, as if expecting him to make the first move. But Nicholas, despite allegedly being the more mature one of the pair, pressed his mouth into a flat line and looked elsewhere. After another long moment, Robin put the mug down on the kitchen counter rather heavily, and returned to his room.

And Nicholas wouldn't unwind again even for Dave's sake.

ten

It finally happened the very next morning. Dave's world collapsed.

Dave and Vittorio had planned a trip out to the camping store at Enoggera, and Dave figured he'd better take Nicholas and Robin as well, rather than leave them to stew in each other's company. The four of them made a rather subdued group wandering the aisles while Dave advised Vittorio on the Agostini family's camping needs. Each of them were wheeling trolleys, as Dave took the opportunity to collect a few necessaries for himself as he went.

It didn't take long before Robin and his smartphone hung back long enough to lose them, and then at least Nicholas relaxed a little.

"What's happened between you two?" Vittorio asked in his blunt Italian-Australian way.

Nicholas shrugged in reply with a weak wry smile. "Dave will tell you it's the same old same old. We can't agree to disagree."

"You'll be all right," Vittorio concluded.

"Both too stubborn for our own good," Nicholas said.

"You'll work it out."

"I don't know …"

They'd reached the aisle of day packs and hiking packs, which lit Vittorio up like it was Christmas. "So here we have," said Dave, "your basic backpack porn …"

That at least earned him a guffaw from Nicholas and a chuckle from Vittorio. And after Vittorio had found himself the perfect backpack, the three of them wound on through the store, and finally met a marginally more sociable Robin at the registers. A short while later they were in the car park, shifting their purchases into their vehicles. Once that was done, a brief silence stretched.

Vittorio, meaning well, offered, "Robin, do you want to come home with me and help me organise all this? I'm sure Denise would be happy for the company. The girls have been nothing but mischief lately, but they always behave for you."

Robin scowled, though he answered politely enough, "No, thank you, Uncle Vittorio, but please say hello to Denise for me."

"All right, no worries."

Dave shook Vittorio's hand, and conveyed his thanks for the thought with a feeling expression.

He was aware of Nicholas standing a little way behind him, his stance a bit off-kilter. "I wish my father were here," Nicholas commented rather vaguely.

"Not long now," Dave reassured him, checking that the Cruiser's rear door was firmly fastened, and mentally trying to do the maths. Was Richard due to arrive in ten days now, or nine?

"David –" Nicholas was reaching towards him, helplessly too far away.

Dave was already turning towards him, was already starting to fear – when Nicholas seemed to just fold down into a wrecked heap on the ground. For a millisecond, for an eternity, Dave stared in horror.

Then – *"Nicholas!"* – he was crouching at Nicholas's side, hands trying to secure him, gaze desperately trying to find the things he needed to know, the things he needed to do.

Nicholas's hands were at his head, and he let out a wail that seemed all the more stricken for being strangled.

Robin echoed the wail, louder and stronger, and then cried out his name – *"Nicholas!"*

Dave kept one hand on Nicholas – he couldn't not be hanging on – but his other hand was fumbling for his phone.

Vittorio was a step ahead of him. Even in the middle of that moment, Dave didn't forgive himself for that. Vittorio had already found his mobile, dialled 000, was saying, "Ambulance, please. *Immediately.*"

Robin looked like he was about to fall over himself, or fall onto Nicholas – and Vittorio was one step ahead of Dave there, too – Vittorio suddenly slid an arm around Robin's waist to secure him and spun around with his momentum to keep him clear. All the while, Vittorio was calmly explaining the situation, giving Nicholas's name, and even that of his neurologist.

Dave's attention returned to the only place it belonged.

Nicholas moaned miserably, clutching at his head, and then one eye peered up at Dave through his fingers, blearily, warily.

"Help's on the way," Dave reassured him. "Hang on, all right? Help is on the way."

Nicholas tried to say something, maybe only Dave's name, maybe something important, and Dave tried desperately to read it in his eyes instead. When he couldn't, Dave resorted to the only words he knew to say.

"Hang in there, Nicholas. Stay with me, all right? Help will be here very soon, I promise."

There was the sound of running feet as others gathered, urgent questions, Robin's distraught sobs and pleas, and above all the sound of Vittorio's calm commanding voice. Thank God for Vittorio. It turned out that Dave wasn't much use after all, so thank God for Vittorio.

Nicholas's eyelids drooped a little, and maybe he wanted to escape the pain, but Dave was determined to keep him awake and aware. "Stay with me, Nicholas, don't leave me, all right?"

Dave eased Nicholas into a more comfortable position, cradling him gently, supporting his poor head, making sure he could breathe.

"I know it hurts. I know it hurts, but I love you," Dave said. "I love you so much, I know you know that, I know you love me, oh God I know it hurts but God please don't leave me …"

Nicholas was looking up at him rather piteously – and then, horribly, his expression slid away and he became blank. Not even peaceful; just blank.

"Please don't leave me, *please* – I'll do *anything* –"

There were sirens.

"Help's coming. D'you hear that? Help's coming. Hang on, Nicholas. Hang onto me, hang on for me. *Please.*"

Then Dave himself had to let go. Firm hands pried Nicholas away from him, and he had to let go. He could be brave enough to do that much, at least. "Aneurysm," he blurted, and was about to say more –

"We've been briefed, sir." The medics were careful but brisk. They established Nicholas was alive. They needed to get him to hospital. That was all. Dave crouched there, watching, but within moments Nicholas was bundled neatly onto a gurney, oxygen mask over his face, eyes closed peacefully as if there were no pain any more and there never had been … Dave's heart wrenched in his chest.

"Sir?" one of the medics asked as they gently hefted Nicholas into the ambulance.

"I'm his husband," Dave said clearly and strongly.

"Come with us, then."

He climbed aboard and sat where they showed him. He rested a hand on

Nicholas's shoulder.

At the last moment he thought to look back out through the doors – before they closed he saw Robin sagging in Vittorio's arms, crying his eyes out – and above that was – oddly – Vittorio's smile shining confidently, almost proudly, as if knowing all would be well.

"All will be well," Dave murmured to Nicholas, who surely couldn't hear him. "All will be well," he repeated, knowing that it mattered anyway. "Nicholas – husband – all will be well. I promise."

The ambulance ride was relatively quiet, oddly insulated as they were from the sirens. One of the medics drove with a reassuring economy of effort, while the other sat in the back, monitoring Nicholas, and relaying information to the hospital, occasionally asking Dave questions, all of which he knew the answer to, thank God. He soon discovered that Dr Williams, Nicholas's consulting neurologist, was on a shift at the hospital, and he'd be making ready to receive him. If emergency surgery was required, then it would be someone else undertaking it – but informed by the man Nicholas had chosen and talked with at length.

"Tell him thank you, if you can," Dave asked, as at least one knot of the thousand in his gut relaxed a little.

"Will do," was the medic's reply.

"We're almost there," the driver added.

"Thank you," Dave said again. If this was going to happen, then – short of Nicholas actually having been in the hospital at the time he collapsed – it was happening in almost the best way it could, with the best chances of them all pulling him through. Dave didn't like the fact that Nicholas was unconscious, but at least that meant he wasn't suffering. Dave gently firmed his hold on Nicholas's shoulder, then bent over to press a kiss to that pale forehead, looking bare now with most of the thick dark hair swept off to one side. This was probably the quietest moment they'd have together for some while now. "Nicholas," he whispered – and then he ran out of words, no longer in that urgent place he'd been only moments before, where he'd blurted out any reassuring nonsense or urgent plea that crossed his mind. Dave sighed. "Nicholas …"

Minutes later, an eternity later, they were at the hospital, and Nicholas was being slid out of the ambulance on his gurney – and chaos erupted, though it probably only seemed like chaos because Dave wasn't initiated into the whys and wherefores of what was happening. There was a lot of clipped talk back and forth, cold clinical talk about the man he loved, and at some point in some corridor Dave was held back from following any further. He watched yearningly, drinking in every moment in which he could see his husband, until at last too soon Nicholas was gone, and the nurse who'd held Dave's arm finally released him with a pat, and said, "He's in good hands, Mr Taylor, the very best – and for you, for you there are forms to complete, so very many forms."

Dave dragged his gaze away from the empty corridor, the closed door, and found that he could, after all, summon a weak kind of smile. "Oh good," he responded a bit hollowly.

And the nurse chuckled appreciatively under his breath and led Dave away.

He'd hardly even worked his way through the first two bits of paperwork before Denise, Vittorio and Robin were there. Dave stood, letting everything fall away, and he walked forward into an intense group hug. They all just held each other for a long hard moment, heads tucked in together – but then of course the others wanted news, they needed to know, so they each stepped back a little, just a little, except Robin who clung like a limpet to Dave's side. Dave kept him there with a comforting arm around his shoulders.

"What's happening?" asked Denise. "Is he – ?"

"He's being diagnosed," Dave said, saving her from saying any other kind of D word. "He's in Intensive Care. Dr Williams is with him. There's no visitors allowed, of course."

She looked gobsmacked. "Diagnosed? Don't they *know*? Isn't it *obvious*?"

"Well, no. They have to be sure. No point in doing brain surgery if it turns out to be a migraine."

Denise turned to Vittorio. "But you said –"

Dave didn't want to hear that either. "I know. We all saw it. Looked like a – like a stroke." He swallowed hard over that bitter word. "But when a CT scan confirms that, and confirms the location – then it'll be surgery of one sort or another."

The four of them fell silent contemplating this enormity.

Finally Denise said briskly, "Well, we're here for as long as it takes, all right? Whatever you or Nicholas need, we're here for you."

"Thanks, that's great. That's really great. But it's gonna take a while, and there won't be much to do other than wait."

"That's all right." She left a beat. "They were … hopeful, right?"

"I dunno. No one's said much yet." Dave looked around at the others, and realised he was probably going to end up reassuring them more than being reassured. "Look, I don't like that he was unconscious even in the ambulance, but we got him here quickly – thanks to Vittorio – and nothing worse happened. As far as I know, there's been no complications. So let's go with 'cautiously optimistic', yeah? That's how his doctor always put it. If we got him here in time – which we did – we could be cautiously optimistic."

Robin sagged heavily against Dave and muttered, "It's my fault, though, isn't it, it's all my fault."

"No," they soothed. "No, of course not." And Dave asked, "Why would you even think that?"

"Because, you know, I was always arguing with him about – well, you know what. I was always – making him mad."

"It is *not* your fault, Robin. You don't even need to think about going there. We always knew that if this was gonna happen, it was gonna happen, no matter where we were or what was going on."

"I guess," Robin whispered doubtingly.

"I'm just thanking God we weren't out at the waterhole or somewhere, a hundred clicks from help."

Robin nodded, though he lacked conviction.

"What about his family?" asked Vittorio. "When are you going to call them?"

"It's the middle of the night in England. At first I thought I'd give it a couple of hours, cos maybe we'll have some news by then. But then I figured Richard might want to catch the first flight out in the morning, and we should give them as much notice as possible." Dave tightened his hold on Robin for a moment. "What d'you reckon? Do you think your grandfather will want to drop everything and come over right away?"

"Yes." Robin was still wide-eyed and tear-stained, but seemed marginally more comforted.

"Good. Nicholas will like that, too. So we'll do what we can to make that happen." Dave took a breath. What hadn't he thought of yet? There were probably a thousand things, and he wanted to get things sorted as much as he could so that once Nicholas was back in the wards, Dave would be free to just be with him. "Oh. Where are Zoe and Bethan?" he asked.

"At my mother's," Vittorio replied in easy tones. "She loves having them all to herself, so don't worry about them, Dave. You don't have to worry about anything other than you and Nicholas, all right?"

Dave looked at him feelingly. Gratefully. "All right. And please say thanks to Maria for me."

Denise took Robin off to the cafeteria to fetch them all drinks, and Dave took the opportunity to call Simon. It was midday in Australia, which meant it would be three in the morning in England. Simon's habit was to always be up by six, but early starts wouldn't make a three a.m. phone call any easier to deal with. Still, Dave figured they'd expect him to call, under the circumstances.

Dave felt he had himself pretty much together, and he tried to make the phone call as brief, calm and informative as it needed to be. He still must have sounded shaken, though, because Simon ended up reassuring him. "You've done everything we could have wanted for Nicholas, and more besides. Thank you, David."

"Well, there's no call to be thanking me yet. If there ever will be!"

Simon took a breath, as if about to say something before changing his mind. After a moment he said, "I'll go and tell Richard myself now, David, then I'll call you or text you with the details. I'm sure you're right: he'll want to be there with Nicholas just as soon as he can."

"No worries. One of us will come pick him up at the airport. If I'm needed here, it'll be Denise or Vittorio, all right? Just let us know when."

"Oh," said Simon, "and what about Robin? Is Robin all right?"

"Yeah, as much as can be expected. Um … he and Nicholas had been disagreeing about something – I mean, not when it happened, but over the past few days – so Robin's a bit upset about that. Otherwise, he's coping."

"Good. Please give him our love – give everyone our love – and reassure Robin and Nicholas that Richard will be there just as soon as he can."

"No worries," said Dave. And with that they said their farewells and hung up.

Dave took a long breath and tucked the phone away in his pocket. Then he sat back down to do some more paperwork – though he suspected most of it was just a ploy to distract him and keep him out of the way. Although that was proved to be the cynical view when the nurse came to fetch the first completed form, quickly reading through it and verbally double-checking that Nicholas hadn't eaten anything since an early breakfast.

Dave was through the third form and on to the fourth before he thought to ask. "Vittorio."

"Mmm?"

"Why were you smiling? I mean, when we were in the ambulance about to leave. I looked out and you were smiling."

"It's not that I wasn't unhappy about Nicholas," Vittorio began.

"No, I know that." Dave looked at him. "I didn't take it the wrong way. It just made me wonder."

"Well," said Vittorio, settling down into his seat and even now faintly echoing the smile. "I was just remembering how you used to go bright red, like a tomato, every time you called Nicholas your husband or said you were his. So much has changed since then, Dave. So much has changed, and for the better."

Dave nodded, and bent his head over the paperwork again. But he couldn't quite focus on the words or the lines. He frowned over them some more, and tried it without his glasses, but it was hopeless. He put it aside for now.

After a while, in a very small voice, he admitted, "I'd give anything to go back to this morning, and keep things exactly the way they were."

Vittorio nodded, too, and reached for a moment to grasp his hand. "I know, Dave. We all would."

Dr Williams appeared soon after Denise and Robin returned with polystyrene cups of coffee and tea, and bottles of water. Dave stood to meet the neurologist and shake his hand. "Is he all right?" Dave blurted, not bothering with the social niceties.

The slightest pause – which could signify anything – before Dr Williams replied, "There's been no change, no worsening of his condition. May I speak freely?" he asked, with a tactful glance at the others.

"They're family," Dave said. Though he was glad enough when Denise went to put an arm around Robin's shoulders.

"We've done a CT scan, and there has been quite a bleed, I'm afraid, but it's exactly where we'd expect it based on his history. It's as accessible as these things can be, and we've already relieved some of the pressure. But Nicholas is still unconscious, David." And Williams waited for a response.

Dave nodded curtly to indicate his understanding. He knew that Nicholas's chances would have been far better if he'd remained conscious.

"We have one of the best neurosurgeons available – and I mean one of the best in the country, not just in Brisbane. She and I have consulted at length, and with other specialists, and we've decided that early surgery is called for under the circumstances. If he were conscious, we'd wait for twenty-four hours to allow for the swelling to subside. But, in fact, Nicholas is being prepared for surgery now."

Dave nodded again, unable to trust his voice. Though he wanted to know –

"We've decided on clipping," Dr Williams continued, as if he knew exactly what Dave was thinking.

That meant a craniotomy. Brain surgery. Dave swayed a little, but Vittorio was there at his elbow.

"As you know, it's a more invasive method than coiling, but there are also lower rates of recurrence and re-bleeding."

Dave managed to say, "I know." What the doctor was tactfully not spelling out was that there were higher risks from the operation itself with clipping, though the long-term effects were better than with coiling. If Nicholas came through this, then he'd be best placed for a good recovery and less danger of any future ruptures. "I understand," Dave offered.

"Of course Nicholas talked through the options with me at some length, so he knew what he'd be facing. I feel confident he'd understand our decision."

"No, that's fine," Dave said, though his throat felt like it was jammed up badly. "Shouldn't you be with him?"

"Yes, I'll be there throughout. But do you have any questions?"

"How long?"

"The operation might take up to six hours, David. If there's anything to report I'll let you know, but I'm afraid you'll have rather a wait."

"That's all right," he said roughly. "I have to be here."

"Nicholas will be glad of it," Dr Williams reassured him. And then, with a kind nod and a half-smile for them all, he turned and left.

Dave sat down.

The others sat down, too, and were silent – though Dave suspected that was because they knew a hell of a lot less than Dave did about exactly what was happening and what the ramifications were. Even if Nicholas survived the operation and the next couple of days, there was a good chance he'd suffer some loss of function, whether physical or mental. There was a good chance he'd change in some ways. Though of course he'd still be Dave's husband, and Dave his, so the fundamental things would remain regardless.

And Nicholas hadn't been scared in those last moments. He'd known what was happening, and Dave had hated the way Nicholas had gone kind of blank, but he wasn't scared. He'd peered up at Dave quite calmly, all things considered.

"He wasn't scared," Dave said, conscious for once of thinking out loud.

"Of course not," said Denise. "And you know what? It'll be all right."

"Will it?" he asked, wondering how she could possibly know that.

"Whatever happens, it'll be all right, Davey. You've both been so wise. No unfinished business, that's the secret. Nicholas was always about seizing the day – and what with you being you, Dave, you both lived your lives to the full."

"Me being me?" he queried.

"You being such an obliging bloke," she said with a cheerful wink. "No unfinished business. Either way, that works for you."

"Either way," he echoed, unwanted images flickering through his head of what might well be his bittersweet future. Bitter with loss, sweet with memories. "Well," Dave said, conscious not only of himself but of Robin sitting beside him. "Let's not go there just yet. There's every reason to think Nicholas will be fine. Cautiously optimistic, remember?"

"Oh, absolutely," Denise and Vittorio agreed. "Cautiously optimistic, it is!"

Dave called Simon back – and then spoke to Richard about the surgery. They both agreed it was a good decision, and reassured each other it would all work out well. Then Simon came back on the line with details of when Richard's flight would arrive, early the following evening, Australian time.

Afterwards, Dave called Charlie and broke the news. Charlie was silent for long moments, and Dave kept him company throughout. And then Charlie announced, "I'll be there tomorrow, mate."

"Of course," Dave replied. "I'm guessing I'll be here at the hospital, but if you go to the house first, you've still got the keys, right?"

"Right." Charlie seemed preoccupied with something, which was hardly surprising, so after Charlie asked Dave to call back with any significant news and Dave agreed, they ended the call.

And then all Dave had to do was sit back down and wait. Doing nothing could be the hardest thing of all.

Robin soon distracted himself with his phone, putting his earbuds in to listen to his music while browsing the net and tweeting to his friends. He seemed to have friends globally, because no matter what time it was he always had someone to exchange messages with.

Whether deliberately or not, Vittorio also took the opportunity to slip down more comfortably on the low couch and doze off with his head back, peacefully snoring. Denise and Dave shared a wry look.

"What should we do with them?" Dave quietly asked. "I mean, if it's gonna be six hours. If I'm remembering right, it'll be at least four. Should we send Vittorio and Robin off to Maria's as well? No point in everyone hanging around if they don't need to."

"Let's play that by ear. See how they go. I'm sure they'd rather be here if they can, and we can always get them to run errands if they look like going stir-crazy."

"Errands?" Dave asked, feeling absolutely blank.

Denise huffed a laugh. "Fetching phone chargers for you and Robin, for a start!"

"Good thinking."

"And we will have to eat at some point. I know you'll tell me you don't feel like it," she added, overriding his protest, "but you have to keep your strength up for later, for when Nicholas needs you."

Dave shifted forward on his seat so as to talk to her more confidentially, and Denise shifted likewise. "Look, I have to tell you how great Vittorio was. I know you know that already, but …"

She gave him a soft grin. "Always good to hear it again."

"And it turns out I was useless," Dave continued even as he rolled his eyes in impatience at his own self-pity. "If it wasn't for Vittorio phoning for the ambulance –"

"You'd have done it if you had to, of course you would. But you didn't have to. You took care of Nicholas instead."

Even so. Dave had expected more of himself. Richard and Simon and the rest of Nicholas's family had expected more from him, too.

"You've done your bit," Denise added in bolstering tones, "and chances are good you'll have more of that to do."

"What's my bit, then?"

"Making him happy. Nicholas has been living the dream these past seven years, that's been perfectly obvious. That's what counts. Not who was first to dial triple zero."

Dave sighed, and dropped his head, and thought for a long moment. But then, he'd never hidden anything from his oldest friend. "Denny. Chances are I'll lose him. You know that, right? I'm hoping for the best. But I faced this a long time ago. Chances are he won't come back from this."

Denise leant forward and wrapped her arms around his shoulders, tucked her head in close to his. "I know, Davey. I know, my darling. I've done my homework, too. But whatever happens, we'll deal with it, all right? You won't be alone, no matter what."

"I know," he whispered, scarily close to tears.

"And you'll always know you did everything you possibly could. You loved him as thoroughly as he ever wished for. No one in the world can ask more from you than that."

"Denny …"

She heard or maybe felt the tremor, and withdrew a little to look at him directly. "But we need to be brave for now, all right, Davey love? For Robin's sake, if nothing else. We need to go with 'cautiously optimistic'."

"I know." He nodded, and let a shudder run through him, and then he was fine again. Or fine enough. Like Denise said, he'd deal with it. He'd been preparing to do that for seven years now.

eleven

After an eternity – Vittorio told Dave later that it had been just under five hours – Dr Williams finally appeared and walked towards them with a pleasantly neutral expression. Dave stood, cold with dread, hot with hope. The others stood beside him, Robin clinging to one arm and Denise holding his other hand, with Vittorio bracing them both up. Dave nodded wordlessly at the doctor in a greeting, a query, an affirmation. *It's okay, I'm ready. Whatever it is, I'm ready.*

Dr Williams looked at them all with a friendly glance, and then at last said, "Nicholas has come through the operation very well."

They all sighed and sagged in relief.

"*But*," Dr Williams added, "we're not out of the woods yet."

Dave nodded again, indicating that he should continue.

"The clipping was successful, and we were able to remove all the excess fluid. There was no sign of any other irregularity. Nicholas is breathing well on his own; in fact, all his vitals are quite acceptable. He's stronger than he looks," Williams added with a slight smile.

"Yes," Dave managed to say. He remembered his own satisfaction with that discovery, so many years ago.

"The next twenty-four hours will be crucial. To be honest, the next three or four weeks will bring plenty of challenges. But for now, let's concentrate on this one day at a time."

"Yes."

"We're going to maintain an induced coma overnight, to enable him to rest, to assist in reducing the swelling. In the morning, if Nicholas seems in as good a state as he is now – and certainly if there's been any improvement – then we'll slowly bring him around."

They all looked at each other, on a sudden surge of hope.

"I must warn you, though," Williams continued in heavy tones, "not to expect too much. We won't be able to assess for a while if there's been any long-term damage and, even if there hasn't, Nicholas will probably seem quite dazed and slow to respond. He will probably be confused at where he finds himself, even though he's anticipated this for years. Don't be too disheartened. And I know I can rely on you all to respond kindly and calmly."

Dave's heart thudded urgently. "Does that mean we can see him?"

"David, I want you to come through to the ICU and sit with him overnight. Will you do that?"

He frowned, wondering why there was even a question. "Yes, of course."

"I'm afraid I can only have one of you through there, but I think it's important. I can't cite any empirical evidence, but to have you sitting with him, holding his hand, talking to him – in my view, it can only aid his recovery."

Dave blanched. "*Talk* to him?"

Denise tightened her grip on his hand. "You'll know what to say, mate."

"No, I, uh … Words were never my strong suit, you know?"

"You're underestimating yourself," Denise advised.

"Even your presence will be beneficial, David," Dr Williams said, "but your voice as well would be even more so."

Robin pushed close to murmur, "You can tell him something from me, Uncle David. You can tell him how much I love him, and you can tell him I'm sorry for arguing with him all the time."

Dave looked at Robin directly. "Yeah, I'll tell him that. And you know he'd want me to tell you it's okay, and he loves you, and he's sorry, too, right?"

"Yeah, I know …"

"Good," the doctor replied, rather more briskly. "Have you eaten at all, David?"

"Not really."

"Well, let your family take you up to the cafeteria for a sandwich and a juice to see you through, and then come to the ICU. I'll meet you there."

Denise insisted that she'd stay in the waiting area overnight, just in case Dave needed her for anything – "Anything at all." After some verbal rambling among them all, it was agreed that Vittorio would take Robin and go to his mother's to join her and the girls. Robin veered wildly between relief at escaping the hospital for a while and guilt at leaving Nicholas, but the others pointed out to him at length that he wouldn't be able to see Nicholas until later the next morning even in the best case scenario, and he finally allowed himself to be persuaded.

Eventually Vittorio and Robin left, after hugging Dave warmly, and then

Denise accompanied him up to the ICU. Dave introduced himself to the nurse at the station, with Denise hanging onto his hand as if unwilling to let him go.

The nurse welcomed Dave with a smile. "I can take you to Mr Goring Taylor now. Dr Williams is already with him." Though she cast a doubting glance at Denise.

"I promise I won't cross the threshold if you'll let me take a peek," Denise said. "I just want to see for myself he's still with us, yeah?"

Dave backed this up with a hopeful expression, suddenly realising that he would actually appreciate having Denise there. God only knew whether Denise had this in mind as well, but it occurred to Dave that he might find the initial sight of a post-op Nicholas rather shocking. Denise could shore him up through that, and from then on he reckoned he'd be fine. He thought he could cope with anything, just so long as he could get his bearings first.

The nurse only took a moment to agree, and then beckoned them down the ward. It seemed that each patient was in their own separate room, though the walls along the main corridor were all glass, presumably so the nursing staff could easily keep an eye on everyone. Part of Dave relaxed at the thought that whatever kind of one-sided conversation he had with Nicholas that night wouldn't be overheard – and it was probably only fair on the other patients that they didn't need to suffer through his illiterate ramblings on top of everything else.

And then they were there. The nurse indicated a particular doorway, and Denise came to a halt just outside – and Dave did, too, clinging as hard to her hand as ever she'd clung to him.

Nicholas lay in a wide hospital bed, on his back and neatly arranged – far more neatly than he slept normally – with the bed propping his head and torso up at an angle. An oxygen mask covered much of his face, and tubes ran into or out of his left hand. A drip was, presumably, providing nutrition, which was surely a good sign. Dave braced himself to look further – and saw a pristine bandage wrapped around Nicholas's head, with a tumble of dark hair poking out the top. The area around Nicholas's eyes seemed a little puffy, a little bruised. But that was it. All right, Dave probably didn't need to fear witnessing anything truly horrific, and anyway he would bear even that if he had to. It wasn't that Dave didn't know something about anatomy and biology.

There were monitors and other machines to either side of the bed, and Dr Williams was carefully considering one and taking notes on a clipboard. He finally looked up and said, "Come in, David. And Denise, isn't it? You can come in for a moment, too, if you wish. I hope you'll find Nicholas's condition reassuring."

"Yes," she said.

"He's pale," Dave blurted. And it was true. Under Nicholas's usual softly-burnished tan, he seemed utterly white. "Has he – Did he – lose a lot of blood or something?"

"Not so much that we had to give him a transfusion. The fluid –" Williams tapped his pen against the drip bag – "will not only keep him hydrated and nourished but also help him replenish his own stocks, as it were."

"He looks fine, all things considered," was Denise's verdict.

Dave was more hesitant. "Dunno. He looks … tired." Perhaps it took a husband's scrutiny to see that while Nicholas appeared to be resting peacefully, he still looked drawn as if having been through an ordeal. Which he had, after all.

"Are you going to be all right?" Denise asked Dave, obviously concerned.

"Of course I am. Hanging out with Nicholas … What else should I be doing?"

She grinned at him, and pressed a rare kiss to his cheek. "You're such a good bloke, Dave." Then she let him go. "Well. You know where I'll be if you need me. For anything, all right?"

"Anything at all," he agreed. And he managed to press a kiss to her cheek, too, before they parted.

Soon enough, Dave was sitting at Nicholas's bedside, and he was carefully shaping his own hand around Nicholas's, trying not to jar him or startle him. Dr Williams had beat a tactful retreat, and while the door to the room was open, Dave was pretty much alone with Nicholas. Still, it took him forever to find his voice.

"Hey, Nicholas," he finally murmured roughly, softly. "Hey, it's me. Dave – David. I guess – I guess if you can hear me, then you just heard Dr Williams telling me all over again to talk to you. Which is probably, like, the last thing you want, really. You probably just want to sleep quietly, don't you? So I'm not gonna keep this up all night, but I'll be here regardless, all right? I'll be here with you."

Dave sighed. "I've missed you. I've missed working things out with you. Isn't that crazy? I kept thinking, oh, if only I could talk to Nicholas about Nicholas being – well, being in surgery, for instance. Nicholas would have the right ideas about what to do. You know, about you. Being in surgery … Oh never mind, I don't even know what I was thinking, really."

A pause stretched into a silence. Surely he wasn't done already? Nah, he could manage more than that. He could at least get the easy stuff out of the way. "Um, so Robin wanted me to tell you how much he loves you, and he's sorry. I told him you loved him, and you were sorry, too. I know you wouldn't have wanted this happening while you and he were disagreeing, but I also know you've already forgiven each other and all that, so let's consider that sorted, yeah? And then I'll just need to convince Robin it's okay. I'm sure he'll see that once he's over the shock.

"Oh, and your father is on his way. He'll be on a plane already. I called Simon, and they were going to make sure Richard would be on the first possible flight. So you'll have your wish. D'you remember saying you wanted to see him? Right before all this happened. I guess maybe you felt it coming, did you? Anyway, he'll be here tomorrow evening. They're going to wake you up tomorrow morning, and you'll be able to see me and Robin, and then Richard will be here. I know that'll make you happy.

"I don't know if they'll let Denise and Vittorio in, not while you're still in the ICU, but they've been here all day with me. Denise is still here. She's going to sleep on the couch in the waiting room so she'll be here if we need her. I know you know they love you. They love you like family. You have to –"

Dave looked at his husband, the dark eyelashes casting a long shadow down those pale cheekbones. He'd have loved to reach up and brush fingertips across those plump pink lips, but didn't trust himself to be gentle enough. Perhaps it was only in his imagination – he should have checked with Dr Williams – but Dave thought any touch might reverberate through Nicholas and hurt him. When his very brain was tender, it seemed that any sensation at all would be too much.

Well, instead he could cradle Nicholas's hand, and keep talking, he supposed. Not that he could remember what he'd been going on about. "What else is there to talk about? God, it seems like forever ago, but it was only this morning when we were talking for real, and you were answering back. And I've missed you since then, I've missed you so much.

"But that's all right. I don't want you feeling bad about that. I guess you'll be in here for a few weeks, and of course I'll come visit you every day, but the nights are going to be so long without you, that bed of ours will feel so empty."

Dave made himself stop and regroup. "I should be talking about happier things. I should be giving you reasons to come back to me. If you need reasons."

And then he frowned over that for a while. Nicholas slept quietly, and the monitors hummed along. Dave did some hard thinking.

"Nicholas," he eventually said. "You once told me … It's a long time ago now, but it really struck me. Back when we were first together, it must have been, out at the waterhole. You once said that … that under some circumstances … you'd prefer to die."

Dave sighed, and let that sit between them.

"And, you know … it's not like I don't understand. I really do, actually. If it were me, in some situations I'd be hoping that you – or Denise – would be brave enough to pull the plug. So, anyway, if that's what I'm meant to be talking to you about … Is it? I don't know. Maybe Dr Williams even … maybe he means for this to be me saying a proper goodbye to you. D'you think?"

Dave traced a careful fingertip along the back of Nicholas's hand, from each of the four knuckles to his wrist and back again. "Can you tell? From the inside, I mean. Can you tell how things are going to be? What you've lost and what you've kept." He took a breath, staring down at that beloved hand. "If you can tell already, and if you're sure it'll be unbearable for you … then I can be brave enough to let you go. I can. It'll be the hardest thing ever, but I'll do it. All right?"

Dave risked a glance up at that beautiful face, and wondered if he was imagining that Nicholas looked as if he were listening. Dave cleared his throat, and tried to continue – but couldn't until he'd dropped his gaze to Nicholas's hand again. "If you want to slip away … or if you want to stay asleep so long they give up on you … then I'll understand. I promise. I want what's best for you."

He let that sit between them, too. He wanted Nicholas to know – if indeed he was hearing any of this – that Dave was serious.

But then he took a deep breath and said, "If you want to stay, though, under any conditions at all, then God I'd give anything for that. *Anything.* I don't care, d'you hear? If you're not entirely the same man you used to be – I don't care. You'll always be Nicholas. You'll always be my husband. And I'll always want you in my life. I *promise*. No matter what."

Dave took off his glasses and put his head down then; he rested his forehead lightly against their joined hands, and perhaps he got a little more than damp-eyed for a while.

Finally, though, Dave found the wherewithal to lift his head and look lovingly at Nicholas, and even crack a wavering kind of smile. "Anyway, don't you remember? We have opals to find, and butterflies, too, and sunsets to watch. We've got family and friends to love, and people to share the Outback with, and our godchildren to have fun with and learn from – and then hand back at the end of the day. We've got each other to take care of, and love – I love you so much, you know – and oh God, there's plenty of sex to have, too. Or hey, there's plenty of kissing and cuddling to be done, even if … even if we can't –" He didn't follow that thought to its logical conclusion, for fear of Nicholas discovering another reason to slip away.

"And there's songs to be sung, and stories to be told, and there always will be. There's so much life we've yet to live, Nicholas. I mean, don't come back to me unless you really want to, but … d'you remember Monica Baldry made up that rap song about us?" And Dave softly sang, "*Nick is his man till death do us part; They got two bodies, one soul, they got one heart.* Wasn't that cool? That was just about the most perfect trip … And there'll be more like that, I reckon. I'd love to share them with you."

Dave soon found himself spinning a yarn about another awesome trip they might take, and all the adventures they might have, the wonders they might see. And then there was another one, and another, each more brilliant than the last, and there were beautiful butterflies to be found and there was sex to be had under the myriad stars, and the marvels of salt lakes and billabongs and cave paintings to visit. Dave talked himself into a stupor, until at last he couldn't help but lay his head down beside his hand joined to Nicholas's … and in his dreams they were holding hands, and they took flight together into a sky as beautiful as an opal, and they soared.

Dave woke confused and bleary with a crick in his neck and something buzzing that shouldn't be. A moment later he realised the latter was his phone, which he'd switched to silent and vibrate, before stuffing it into his jeans pocket.

He carefully lifted his head, and turned a hopeful gaze on Nicholas. There seemed little change, though maybe Nicholas wasn't quite as pale as Dave had expected, maybe he was a little less puffy. A harder look made him think he might be imagining it, but his first impression had been a surprise. Nicholas was still asleep, was still looking untroubled. At least, Dave figured, he wasn't in pain, and that wasn't such a bad bottom line.

His phone started buzzing again, so he hauled it out – glancing towards the corridor a tad guiltily, though there were no witnesses, or none that were conscious, and anyway he'd wanted to be available if Denise or Simon needed him. Dave answered the call – "H'lo" – without checking the display.

"Davey, it's Charlie."

"H'lo, Charlie." Dave looked around at the window, and judged from the paling darkness that it was almost dawn. "Always the early bird, you," he said fondly.

"How is he, mate?"

Dave looked his husband again. "Still asleep. I was, too. Um, he looks kinda the same as last night. At first I thought there's a bit more colour to him, but maybe that's wishful thinking."

"Okay, good. So he's hanging in there."

"Yeah. I guess they'd – they'd have woken me, wouldn't they? If there was anything to tell me. I must have been out of it for two or three hours."

"I've got a song for him, all right, mate? A healing song."

The light outside warmed a little.

"Davey?"

"Yeah, I'm here. Yeah, okay. That's good."

"It's as close as I can tell to his Dreaming. Robin?" Charlie asked. "What do I do with this now?"

"What?" Dave asked, still struggling to wake up properly. "You're at Maria's, Charlie?"

"Nah, I've just got Robin on the other line. It's a convention call, or something. Hang on a sec."

"*Conference* call, Charlie," came Robin's voice. "Morning, Uncle David. Did you tell Nicholas for me?"

"Yeah, I told him, mate," Dave gently replied.

"Good." Then Robin went through a few instructions for Charlie about swiping and tapping and such, all of which was Greek to Dave who still had the old-fashioned kind of keyboard phone.

Not too long after, an Aboriginal chant began in Dave's ear, accompanied by the percussive beat of clapsticks. It was a mesmerising sound, and while it felt changeless it was also strangely hopeful. The same long refrain repeated again and then again – or maybe Charlie just had it on a loop – and in any case it felt oddly familiar to Dave. Before he'd even heard it through once he was already humming along, and after a while he held the phone at a slight distance so perhaps Nicholas could hear something of it, too. Dave began quietly chanting. He didn't understand the words, but he recognised the sort of sounds they made, the vowels and the consonants, and he could copy that well enough.

After a time, Robin said, "Uncle David? If I talk Charlie through sending you the sound file, can you play it to Nicholas, do you think?"

"I guess," Dave replied. "But he's hearing it now, and I'm singing it to him."

"That's enough," said Charlie. "That's everything he needs."

It was fully light outside when Dr Williams appeared not long after, walking in to find Dave chanting softly to Nicholas, trying to sound both soothing and encouraging – though he stopped abruptly as soon as he realised they had company.

The doctor smiled, and said, "That sounded nice."

"It's a healing song, apparently. Something to do with Nicholas's Dreaming. I think he has Butterfly Dreaming."

"Excellent." The doctor checked the various machines and charts, and studied Nicholas himself in between times. Then he made some notes on his clipboard.

Dave wasn't feeling very patient, however. "Is he doing all right?"

Dr Williams smiled at him. "What do you think?"

"Well," said Dave, considering Nicholas again. "He seems pretty much the same to me. Maybe not quite as pale?"

"I thought so, too." Williams studied Nicholas some more – then announced, "We'll try letting him wake up later this morning. Why don't you go tell Denise the good news, and the two of you can have some breakfast. Take your time, there's no rush."

Dave nodded, though he asked, "Then I can come back, right?"

"Of course, David. Then you can come back."

By the time Dave returned, though, something was very different. Dave's heart thudded hard when he realised.

Nicholas was scowling. Rather blearily, it was true, but Dr Williams was sitting by the bed talking quietly, and Nicholas was scowling, looking oddly restless for someone who was barely even moving his face.

"D'you see that, Denny?" Dave whispered.

"Oh that's marvellous!" she whispered back. She stopped at the threshold, and tried to let go of Dave's hand. "Go on, then! Go say hello."

Williams looked around, and beckoned Dave forward. He went with trepidation, more scared now than he'd been since all this began. Eventually he reached the chair he'd been sitting on all night, on the opposite side of the bed than Williams. And he sank to sit down, moving carefully. Not wanting to startle or confuse Nicholas with any unexpected movement. He didn't quite dare reach to take his husband's hand. Instead, into the rustling beeping quivering silence, he said, "Nicholas?"

At which Nicholas scowled some more, and then his gaze wandered haphazardly across to finally settle on Dave. A long moment while Nicholas tried to focus on him, finally squinting a bit, as if he didn't quite dare believe it really was Dave. But then at last he seemed to comprehend or maybe simply accept, and the frown lifted as if by magic and the scowl smoothed away – and one corner of that gorgeous mouth quirked into a smile.

"Nicholas ..." Dave murmured happily, reaching now to gently cradle Nicholas's hand in his own, just as he'd been holding it all night. "Oh Nicholas ... you little beauty. Oh thank God. Thank the Ancestors! Everything's going to be all right."

Nicholas's hand clutched briefly at his, though it seemed to require quite an effort, and then he could be seen to be forming a word. Dave and Dr Williams just waited, letting him take his time. Eventually Nicholas stuttered out, "S-s-song," though the G was more implied than spoken.

Dave burst into a grin. "You heard that? Charlie found it for me. It was a healing song."

Nicholas, however, seemed to want to roll his eyes impatiently. He got about halfway through that and gave up, then tried saying another word. "L-lines …"

"Lines?" Dave only took a moment. "Songlines? Is that what you're saying?"

Nicholas nodded a little, and seemed content enough with that for now.

"Cool," said Dave. "I'm gonna ask you to tell me more about that later, all right? But songlines, yeah? It's so cool you said that."

Nicholas's eyes started slipping closed, though he fought it for a moment, still trying to look at Dave.

"Yes, I think it's time for a nap, Nicholas," Dr Williams said. "You're doing very well, but let's not tire you out on the first day."

"I'll see ya later, Nicholas," Dave added as reassuringly as he knew how. He bent his head to press a kiss to the back of Nicholas's hand, hoping Nicholas would take that sensation with him into sleep. "I'll see you later, husband."

Once he was settled again, no longer lying quite so neatly in the bed, Dr Williams led Dave back out of the room. "Why don't you let Denise take you home for the rest of the morning, David? Have a few hours of sleep."

"But –"

"You'll be more use to him then."

Well, Dave couldn't really argue with that. "Can I come back this afternoon? And his father. His dad's flying over from England; he'll be here this evening. He can come visit, right?"

"Come back at three, David, and his father can join you for a little while this evening. But then I want you to take the night off, all right? Nicholas is in excellent hands here, I promise you."

"I know," Dave agreed with a smile. Denise appeared beside him again, and took his hand ready to take him away. "Thank you, Doctor."

"And thank *you*, David."

After which graciousness, Dave decided to save any further protests for later. With one last look at his beloved husband, Dave turned for home.

Nicholas slept most of the afternoon – a natural sleep, not induced, and apparently occasionally troubled by dreams – but Dave was content to simply sit beside him and hold his hand. Dave figured Nicholas needed most of all to rest, but when he was awake he spent half the time scowling, and even when he looked at Dave his instinctive smile sometimes seemed reluctant. Maybe Nicholas was simply feeling impatient already with where he found himself.

Denise had taken Robin to meet Richard off the plane from England, and brought him directly to the hospital. The reunion of father and son had tears springing even to Dave's eyes.

"Oh my boy," Richard murmured, walking towards the bed as if it were the last stage of a long pilgrimage. Dave brought him around to Nicholas's right side, so Richard could grasp Nicholas's hand without fear of disturbing any of the tubes and such. Richard collapsed to sit on the chair, and murmured again, "Oh my dear boy." The two of them gazed at each other fiercely. Nicholas hadn't said anything since he'd first woken that morning, but his look now spoke eloquently enough. Dave left them to it, and went to regather himself by the nurses' station.

About half an hour later, Richard was gently ushered out by one of the nurses. "He's asleep," Richard said to Dave, his tone full of wonder. "He's truly resting. I've been told to go do likewise. I couldn't sleep on the plane, that's true, but I think I will be able to sleep tonight, now that I've seen him."

"He's doing all right," Dave said, as reassuringly as he could.

"So much better than I'd expected. Better than I dared to hope." Richard looked at him feelingly. "*Thank* you, David. I'm sure we have you to thank for taking such great care of him."

"Well," he responded with an uncomfortable shrug. "I wish I'd done more."

"Nonsense, my boy," said Richard, drawing him into a hug. "You've been everything that we ever hoped for, and more besides."

Neither of them was too proud to cling for a while, but then they took a moment to regroup. Dave cleared his throat. "Why don't we go throw ourselves on Denise's mercy, and see if Vittorio will cook us dinner? I could do with a great big bowl of pasta. Sheer comfort food, you know?"

"I can't imagine anything better," Richard agreed.

twelve

In an astonishingly short period of time – a matter of a few days – Nicholas was well on the way to recovery. He was moved into a room in one of the regular wards, and soon the nurses had him out of bed and sitting up in a chair for a couple of hours each day. He still hardly spoke at all, but it was obvious from his awareness and his reactions that he was as bright and engaged as ever. Dr Williams counselled Dave and Richard to talk to Nicholas, and include him in conversations, just as they normally would when talking with him, and let Nicholas take his own time in choosing to reply. There would be plenty of chances to push a little later, whether gently or firmly, once he was further past the trauma.

"D'you think he's worried that he's lost his abilities, or something?" Dave asked. "Cos I don't reckon he has. I mean, he's still as sharp as a tack. He always knows exactly what's going on."

"Well, like you, I suspect it would be more about the worry than the actuality," Williams agreed. "But let's not push him just yet."

Richard huffed a little under his breath and fondly observed, "He's more than able to convey his meaning, in any case. He's still vain enough to be fretting about the hair you needed to shave off!"

They all had a quiet guilty chuckle about that. Dave regathered himself first. "I'll have to talk to his barber. Later, of course, once the wound's properly healed. Maybe he can visit the house, and come up with some sort of style that makes it look deliberate."

Richard looked at Dave very fondly. "You think of everything."

"Actually, what I'm more worried about," Dave blurted, forever unwilling to forgive himself for his inadequacies, "is the scowling. I mean, what's that about?"

"He never scowls at you, David," Richard pointed out.

"And not at you, either. But pretty much everyone else – even the doc here, and Nicholas has been seeing you for seven years now, hasn't he? I reckon he thinks of you as a friend."

Williams inclined his head. "Thank you. But again, let's wait and see. It might not be anything to worry about in the long-term. It might be a temporary disorientation, or a period of adjustment, or simply impatience."

Richard didn't huff, but actually laughed a little this time. "My dear boy has always tended towards impatience, I'm afraid."

"He's not bad-tempered, though," Dave argued, "and he's not the sort who doesn't like people."

After a moment, the doctor said, "We've talked about the possibility of some changes in behaviour or personality. I suspect from what we've seen that, if there are any, they'll be relatively minor. But it is possible you're seeing a shift in his nature."

Richard turned a worried glance on Dave – who replied before he could think twice about it, "It's not like I mind. Have you really looked at him when he scowls? He's like this great big beautiful thunderstorm."

The other two men laughed heartily.

"He's totally awesome. I'll just keep an eye out for lightning bolts, is all."

Dave experienced a bit of a lightning bolt himself the next morning. He was sitting with Nicholas – and Dave had him to himself for once, as Vittorio had taken Richard and Robin out for the day – and he was reading out loud from one of his own Patrick O'Brian books. There was a passage that had the officers and crew each bonding through the singing of songs, and when Dave came to a chapter break, he put his Kindle aside.

He pondered for a moment, and then met Nicholas's quizzical look. "D'you remember the first thing you said to me when you woke up after the operation?" Dave asked. He left a pause, in which Nicholas lifted his chin slightly in an equivocal answer. "You said 'songlines'. I've been so curious about why. I hope you'll tell me about it one day." Dave left a rather longer pause, though not as if it were an unexpected thing to do. Then he continued, "I was thinking about that song Charlie gave me, too – you know, the one he had me sing to you. Did that have something to do with the songlines?"

Nicholas ducked his head briefly to one side. No.

"No worries," Dave said. "It's not as if I don't like a bit of mystery ..."

Then Nicholas said, very clearly, "I followed the songs back to you."

Dave stared at him, rather startled to say the least.

"I would have found my way back, with or without Charlie."

"Would you?" Dave asked, trying to understand, while also trying not to betray his joyous sense of relief that obviously Nicholas was perfectly able to speak even if he didn't choose to.

"I followed the path of the songlines."

Dave's jaw dropped. "Oh …" Two and two finally started adding up to make seven. "Oh, mate! I think I'm having … Well, never mind that. That's awesome! Now we know you'll always be able to find your way back to me, and probably I will, too, in that case – I mean, find my way to you."

Nicholas nodded a little impatiently, obviously knowing something else was going on.

Dave scrambled for words, for sense. "I think I'm having one of those epi- epif- epicentre things."

Nicholas grinned a bit lopsidedly. "Epiphany."

"Exactly. Oh my God," said Dave. "I've finally figured it out. About the waterhole. I know what I have to do."

Nicholas's grin turned fuller, and he didn't speak again, but his eyes were just *glowing* with love and pride.

"You're brilliant, you know that?" Dave asked. "But what if I have to go do this? *Now*, I mean. Will you be all right if I leave you here for a couple of days, while Richard and Robin are still around to look after you?"

Nicholas favoured him with a half-scowl. But then he ducked his chin in a nod.

"God, I love you *so* much … And it's not like Richard doesn't deserve some proper time with you, yeah?" Dave was already standing, and reaching into his pocket for his phone. "I love you so much, but I've got to call Charlie, all right?"

Of course it was all right. Nicholas smiled at him with an arch kind of sweetness, and his long fingers plucked at the Kindle and lifted it – apparently to give himself something to frown at while Dave made his phone call.

Early in the morning two days later, Dave was standing on a low flat hill in the mulga scrub west of Cunnamulla. Charlie and another Indigenous man named Kalti stood with him.

Waiting below them on the plain was a gathering of friends and strangers. Denise was there with the Cruiser, with Bethan and Zoe in the back. Robin had, surprisingly, decided to abandon Nicholas and come as well. His presence might or might not be explained by the fact that Lisa Munroe was there, though he didn't seem to mind that Lisa had brought her partner Debbie. Ted Walinski was there with his Land Rover, and he'd brought Fred Harvey and Mr Teng with him. Mayor Shirley Johns was there, too, accompanied by Henri Wilson, who owned the big station out to the west of the waterhole. The Native Title guy Martin Bandjara had driven from Brisbane overnight to be part of it. And there was a hearteningly large group of Murri from the reserve and elsewhere, too – including Thursday, magnificently attired in native accessories, a headdress, and swirls of paint but otherwise as good as naked.

Dave took a breath. It was vital that he had witnesses, but oh what a disaster this would be if he messed up.

"You right, mate?" Charlie asked.

"Sure." Dave nodded. "Let's do this, yeah?"

"Yeah. Absolutely."

Dave turned to Kalti, and nodded respectfully. "Okay, so if I'm right, your songline brings you here. And mine starts here. So, would you mind singing the song about this place? If you can share it?"

Kalti nodded, took a couple of paces away, and with no further ado launched into a chant which resounded clearly in the cool morning air.

Within moments Dave was grinning, knowing already that they were off to a perfect start. His own song for this place, the very first of the sequence of songs he'd learned, consisted of exactly the same words, and though the tune was slightly different, the two songs belonged together. As soon as he realised that, Dave started singing, too. Kalti's gaze fixed on him – perhaps he had doubted, as surely most of them did – but now he knew. Charlie had withdrawn a little, and remained silent as if making the point that he wasn't driving this, though he was paying close attention. In fact, everyone was watching and listening in varying degrees of surprise and satisfaction – and of course not everyone would get on board even if Dave succeeded in this, but thank the Ancestors he was off to a good start.

"That song," he said when they were done, "the words: they're something about a small plain on a large plain, right? I never realised what that was about, until now, but it's this hill."

"That's good, mate," said Kalti. "That's right. You done good."

144

"Will you come with us, then? Come to the waterhole with us."

Kalti glanced at Charlie, but not like he was seeking permission. "Yeah, mate," he said to Dave. "I'll come."

While they were still on the hill, Dave began murmuring the next song, scanning the land towards the west, looking for the next location on the songline. It had to be somewhere visible, towards which he could navigate. He couldn't immediately think how the song helped him, though, so he quit singing and said to Charlie, "This is about a snake Ancestor gliding over the ground, isn't it?" It wasn't just the words that told him that, but the undulating rhythm.

Charlie considered for long moments, and then suggested, "*Through* the ground, I think."

"*Through* the ground," Dave muttered, wondering how the hell that worked. But when he looked again, he glimpsed something on the horizon that might help. When he adjusted his glasses on his nose and looked again, he saw a slight but sharp dip in the line of the horizon. He pointed this out to Charlie and Kalti. "Like that? See that kind of … valley? It only looks like a notch from here, but could the snake have gone through there?"

"You beauty!" Charlie cried. "That's it, of course!"

"Cool," said Dave. And singing the song under his breath, he strode down to the level ground, and then struck out across the plain. He was aware of Charlie and Kalti following just behind, and then beyond them a convoy of four vehicles lurched slowly into gear and trailed along, accompanied by a goodly number of people on foot.

They covered just under twenty-three kilometres in this way, making for quite a long day. Dave would interpret the songs in terms of what he could see in the landscape, sometimes with help from Charlie, Kalti and Thursday but mostly on his own. There was only one song that completely stumped them all – and when they decided to have faith and strike out in the same general direction, they soon came to a rocky outcrop that had apparently broken apart or collapsed some decades before, but which had probably once been visible from some distance.

The very last song in the sequence was about a frilled-neck lizard Ancestor who had gone to sleep so long ago that now you could only see his back poking out of the ground. Dave had already figured this related to the worn old ridge of rocks that he'd long followed on his way to the waterhole, as the formation did look just like a spine curving up out of the ground and back down again. The pattern of rocks that he used to think of as an arrowhead at one end could instead be interpreted as a frill at half-mast.

"We're almost there," he said to his companions, unable to suppress his excitement. The ridge of rocks pointed them in exactly the right direction to take them up across the rise that would eventually reveal … the wide valley that contained the waterhole.

Dave paused on the crest of the rise in the warm glow of late afternoon sunshine, and let the others catch up with him. Those people in the vehicles climbed out and joined the group, which somehow felt larger than it should be, almost as if it were thick with spirits.

"That's it there," Dave announced, pointing towards where the trees and scrub were thickest. "That's the waterhole." Not that any of them other than Charlie would realise quite what they were looking at, not yet. "Come on!" Dave cried, and he strode down the long slope into the valley.

They all followed after him, and any tiredness was lost in a hubbub of excitement. Soon Dave was standing at the entrance to the waterhole. The vehicles were left parked at a respectful distance, and the people gathered around Dave. He looked at them all, sharing the moment with the people he loved, and the people he respected. The excitement became more of a fully charged hush … and when the timing was perfectly right, Dave turned and led the way down into this beautiful sacred place.

It was more than time to share the beauty with the world. Even the butterflies seemed to agree. Dave hadn't expected them to have emerged from the chrysalis yet, but a kaleidoscope of blue scraps of sky rose to meet them. His companions gasped in wonder, and Robin cried, "Oh, Nicholas!" He added more quietly, "Oh, I wish he were here …"

Soon the odd assortment of people were scattered across the sandy ground by the pool itself, marvelling at the gorgeous colours, revelling in the lush sense of peace which even this large gathering of humans couldn't dispel.

Without the slightest sense of self-consciousness Dave took up the long-familiar stance, and began chanting the first of the songs about the waterhole itself, sharing the story about the Barcoo grunter Ancestor, and his love who fell from the sky. Charlie fell into step beside him, and they worked through the sequence of songs and dances – agreeing with little more than a glance which must be kept secret – while the others settled to sit in a large circle around them.

Once they were done, they were met with hearty cheers and applause, as everyone celebrated with them. Charlie put his arm around Dave's shoulders to squeeze him tight, giving Dave all the kudos, though Dave knew well enough they shared it between them. "There's another few songs that lead away from here," Dave explained, "that take the songline further out to the west. But I reckon we'll save them for next time. Let's just hang out here for what's left of the day, right?"

"Right," everyone agreed with a happy laugh.

Dave sat beside Charlie and watched as Thursday and Kalti set a small fire going and then lay green eucalyptus leaves on it. The leaves created smoke, which Dave knew was intended to cleanse both the area and the people in it, and symbolise a new beginning. The sharp scent of the leaves was itself stimulating; everyone touched by it smiled.

Thursday beckoned Dave into the place where the smoke was thickest, and gestured through it as if covering Dave with smoke from head to toe. Charlie advised, "Slough off what you don't need, mate. Let the smoke take it." Dave felt immeasurably lighter. He closed his eyes, listening to Thursday and Kalti chant a song of renewal.

Eventually the smoke dwindled, and people began stirring, about to get up and start exploring, when instead they fell quiet.

Thursday was stepping through the circle to Dave with a dillybag in his hand. When he reached Dave's side, he lifted a wooden board from the bag, and silently handed it over.

Dave took it carefully, and considered the painting on the one flat surface. As with most traditional Aboriginal images, it showed the landscape from above, from a bird's-eye view as it were. There was something about the shapes this depicted that felt very familiar – and it only took a moment for Dave to twig. "Oh! Oh, that's the waterhole!" He traced the concentric shapes, not quite daring to touch them. God only knew how old this was. "This is the valley, the crater," Dave said, indicating the largest, almost perfectly round circle. "This is the sinkhole, which we're in," he added, gesturing at the ellipse in the centre of the circle. "And this is the pool." It was an irregular shape towards one end of the sinkhole, pretty much exactly matching the pool itself. There were two people sitting by the water, one male and one female. "Are these the Ancestors, then?" he asked Thursday.

The old man nodded. He was looking happy, and very satisfied. When Dave tried to hand back the board, Thursday shook his head and stepped away.

"But –" said Dave.

Thursday drew near again, but only to give him the dillybag. "It's yours now, Dave. You belong in this place."

And Dave could feel himself beaming with joy. He had hoped to prove a point that day. He hadn't even considered that he might receive such recognition. "Thank you," he said, slipping the board safely back into the bag, and cradling it in both arms against his chest. "Thank you."

The gathering settled after that into the happiest picnic there had ever been, with everyone mingling and chatting happily, or wandering around gazing in quiet awe at the natural beauties of the waterhole. The butterflies continued their happy dance in the day's warmth, occasionally deigning to settle on someone's outstretched hand. Robin was taking plenty of photos with his smartphone so that Nicholas could eventually share in it as well.

Charlie was marvelling. "You do belong in this place, Davey. The Ancestor called you to him, before you even knew the songs."

"I guess so," said Dave. It was a mystery he didn't have an answer for, so Charlie's interpretation made as much sense as anything else.

"I knew all the songs," Charlie continued, giving Dave yet another one-armed hug. "I knew all the same songs, and I couldn't find this place. I couldn't do what you just did. I couldn't follow the songlines."

"Oh well. I guess the Ancestor just decided it was time."

"You're a good man, Davey Taylor."

He grinned at Charlie but bashfully shrugged off the compliment – and instead went to talk to Ted Walinski, who was puzzling over some kind of satnav device. "Not picking up a signal?"

"No, not even a weak one." Walinski looked at him a bit sheepishly. "I'm starting to understand now. I thought you were just being …"

"Difficult?"

"Something like that." He gestured at the red and black cliffs that surrounded them. "Maybe the depth of the sinkhole is interfering with the signal. We'd need a satellite to be almost directly overhead."

"Maybe," said Dave. "But I never got a signal from up at ground level, either. This whole area has been kind of … hidden."

Walinski was sceptical, of course. "Are you saying you believe in – ?"

"I guess we'd all explain it in different ways," said Dave.

"We flew over this area, I'm sure we did. The scrub and the trees would have hidden the sinkhole, I guess, but I don't understand why we didn't spot the crater."

Dave shrugged. "I don't have any answers for you that don't involve the Dreaming, and I know how hard that is for a white fella to accept."

Walinski turned to something he felt surer of. "I wasn't wrong about the hematite, though. That's magnificent!"

"It *is* magnificent," Fred Harvey agreed, wandering up to them with a complacent expression on his face. "Well, you've made your point, Mr Goring Taylor, and I think we can promise you that Reddy Eight will be taking great care not to cause this place any harm."

"But you'll still be looking to start mining in the region," Dave confirmed.

"Yes, but with the smallest possible footprint, I can assure you of that."

Dave sighed, though not unhappily. "I'd like to hear that from Elvis Reddy himself, but I don't mind hearing it from you in the meantime."

"I can do you one better." Harvey nodded his head towards where Mr Teng was sitting serenely meditating by the pool. Teng was still in his expensive shirt and trousers, but his shoes and socks were off, and on top of them were neatly piled his suit jacket and tie. "You can hear it directly from the man with the money, just as soon as you'd like to ask him."

"Oh!" Dave wondered why he hadn't guessed that already. "Mr Teng is actually the major investor?"

"Indeed." Harvey grinned at him. "Like I said, Dave, you've made your point. Well played."

And when Harvey offered his hand, Dave shook it with perfect equanimity.

Once Harvey and Walinski had wandered off, Dave looked around to see that Robin had taken Lisa and Debbie over to the wattle, and the young man was standing there watching with Bethan and Zoe while Lisa examined the plant just as thoroughly and excitedly as ever Nicholas had examined the butterflies.

Denise came over to Dave, and rubbed an affectionate hand up his arm. "This place is *beautiful*. No wonder you and Nicholas love it so."

"Yeah," said Dave, "but it was time to share. The butterflies don't seem to mind, anyway."

"They're astonishing!" she said. "I had no idea … I mean, to see them alive …"

"So, we're trying to get this place included in the Aboriginal reserve; the Department has agreed in principle. But we're also going to try to establish the wattle and some of the butterflies near another waterhole on the reserve. If we set that up properly for visitors, then that helps protect this, if you see what I mean. Nicholas and Lisa are paranoid about how fragile the environment is here."

Denise nodded. "Look, I admire you sharing the waterhole with us, Davey, but I think most people would understand you not opening it up as a tourist site, you know?"

He shrugged, feeling a bit reluctant himself. "I guess we'll have to consult the Ancestor about that!" he offered, more than half seriously.

Charlie, who'd been pondering the pool, heard them and came closer. "The Ancestor is dreaming happy," he declared. "You're right. It was time for him to welcome more of us in."

"It wasn't that we ever wanted to be selfish about it," Dave said. "We never thought we were more … well, more entitled to enjoy it than anyone else."

"Of course not," Charlie bracingly replied. "But you wanted to bring it back to life, and that takes time. You weren't in a rush, Davey, and neither should you be. You know, even Nicholas isn't always about seizing the day."

Denise snorted with laughter, in which Dave joined, and the happy sounds of mirth and quiet wonder and Mr Teng chanting a song of his own – all these lovely sounds mingled and rose and danced in the bright air with the butterflies. Everything seemed vivid and alive, and there was a sense somehow that it was all stirring. Sap was flowing through veins, water was welling through rock, and light was sparkling warmth in all it touched. The timeless feel of the waterhole had shifted, as if somehow it had become part of the world again, part of today, part of a story that wasn't yet fully told.

Dave wandered over to Ted Walinski, and said, "Try your GPS again, would you?"

Walinski did so – and after a long moment he received a signal loud and clear. He looked up at Dave in surprise.

Dave nodded, and headed over to Robin. "Do me a favour, mate? Choose your best photo of the butterflies, and try sending it to Nicholas."

Robin looked doubtful, but he didn't argue. He swiped through the images, and then quickly tapped out a text and sent it. His brow shot up once he realised the message had actually gone. A few moments later the phone rang, and Robin answered it. "Hello, Uncle Nicholas! … No, I know they are, they're just *gorgeous*. … Yes, he did it. … No, we're still here, we're at the waterhole. … I know! It's awesome!"

Dave grinned and wandered away, and found a rock to sit down upon. For long moments he watched the others revelling in this place and each other. Charlie and the Mayor were sharing a yarn that made them both laugh; Lisa was showing Teng the wattle; Denise and the girls were teaching Robin a song. Dave hardly dared even think it, but he suspected that somehow he'd just accomplished something that was utterly impossible. It was the most humbling, the most wonderful thing he'd experienced in his *life*.

Well, next to Nicholas's love, of course. Nothing could be more humbling or wonderful than that. But this came pretty darned close.

epilogue

Despite some last minute bravado from Robin about taking a gap year, in response to which the earl carefully did not panic, the two Englishmen headed home as planned in time for Robin to start the new academic year at Oxford. However, there was much talk about the Goring family observing Christmas in Australia that year, or as many of them as could make it, so Nicholas and Dave would be seeing them again soon.

In the meantime, Dave spent every available moment at the hospital, while making sure that everything was clean and ready and comfortable at home for when Nicholas was finally discharged. He figured it couldn't be much longer now, as Nicholas was pretty much mobile – if currently rather slower than he had been, and almost indiscernibly weaker on the left side. Nicholas was using the time as thoroughly as he could, to pursue as much physical rehab as Dr Williams would let him.

Otherwise, the scowls persisted, and Nicholas still didn't speak any more than he had to. Dr Williams never came up with a definitive explanation for this, or at least not in the physical sense, so Dave tried to simply accept it as one of the inexplicable changes he'd been warned about. He knew how lucky he was to have Nicholas with him at all, so it seemed ridiculously ungrateful to wish everything would return to 'normal'. Crucially, when it was just Nicholas and Dave together, then Nicholas relaxed and was happy, and Dave thought it was perfectly clear that Nicholas was just as sharp and clever and *engaged* as he'd ever been. Not to mention just as outrageous.

One afternoon they were hanging out in Nicholas's room quite innocently, and every now and then talking together about nothing much. Dave was slouched back in the chair, and Nicholas was lying in the bed. At some point after a lull in conversation, Nicholas stretched out tall and rolled back his shoulders, first one and then the other, so that Dave's spine lengthened and popped in sympathy.

And then out of the blue Nicholas asked, as if knowing the answer, "Have you been tossing off without me?"

"What?!" spluttered Dave.

"You heard me." Nicholas rolled onto his side and curled up so he could look directly at Dave. "Have you been taking care of yourself … seeing as

I'm not there to take care of you?"

"Well," said Dave, knowing that his cheeks were burning red, "yes, I suppose." He added in a dismissive tone, "A couple of times, that's all."

Nicholas interpreted that to mean "Not so great?"

"Not without you, no," Dave replied quite evenly. What he didn't say was that it had only been about solace, really. Not pleasure. Just a way of feeling less alone in their enormous bed. The joys of being with Nicholas had spoiled him even for wanking. Dave sighed.

"Well," said Nicholas, "I think you should hop up here on the bed, and let me have a try."

Dave just stared at him for a long moment. And then glanced at the door, which was of course held wide open by one of those magnetic mechanisms. People bustled along the corridor, or ambled along, taking the opportunity to stare in at them as they went. At least the walls were solid here in the wards, and not made of glass as they were in the ICU. But still. It was mid-afternoon in a public building, and anyone might walk in on them.

"Come on," said Nicholas, shifting back on the bed so that Dave would have room to lie beside him.

Perhaps spooning would be the easiest way, and wouldn't it be glorious to have Nicholas pressed up close against his back, tucked up tight against him from top to toe, reaching around to wrap his clever loving hand around Dave's cock … Not that Dave was actually thinking about doing this.

"Come on," Nicholas repeated, reaching that very hand out towards him. "I've missed you …"

"Oh my God, you're serious."

"Of course I am. Haven't you missed me?"

"You know I have." Dave frowned at him, and darted a pointed glance at Nicholas's nether regions. "I'd gotten the impression that … you weren't quite fully recovered yet."

"I'm not," came the tart response. "But that doesn't mean I'm incapable of helping you out. And anyway … there's more to miss than orgasms, isn't there?"

"Kissing and cuddling," Dave agreed.

Nicholas patted the bed beside him. "Come on, then, husband."

Dave groaned in frustration and annoyance. "There's no lock on the door!"

"What, and you don't have a backup plan for that … ?"

Oh God! Dave stared at the man, appalled and aroused in equal measure. Then after a long long moment he pushed himself up from the chair, and headed out to the nurses' station.

Luckily one of the nurses they were most friendly with was on duty. Dave paused for a moment, and then when she looked up enquiringly, he leaned in closer to speak confidentially. "Um … is there such a thing as … as a 'Do Not Disturb' sign we can place on the door?"

She gazed back at him for a moment without blinking an eye. "You're not taking advantage of my patient, are you, Mr Taylor?"

"Actually, it's more like I'm the one being taken advantage of." He held up a hand palm-out. "No, that wasn't funny. Or true. To be honest … I doubt we'll be doing more than cuddling, anyway."

"No worries," she said. "Just had to be sure." She reached into a drawer, and came out with something that looked very much like a hotel's 'Do Not Disturb' sign but read 'Private Consultation'. "Here you are. Put this on the door handle. And draw the curtain round the bed, too, at least down the side facing the door. I'll keep an eye out, but I can't promise no one will blunder in."

"That's all right," he said. "I'll take my chances."

"Have fun," she offered with a wink.

He blushed even harder, and retreated in as good an order as he could manage.

Nicholas didn't speak when Dave returned, but just lay there on his back watching as Dave sorted out the sign and quietly closed the door, then drew the curtain down one side and along the foot of the bed. Neither of them liked to feel too enclosed, so he was happy enough to leave the other side open and, while that was opposite the window, they were on too high a floor to be overlooked by anything but the sky.

As Dave took off his glasses and then heeled off his shoes, Nicholas turned onto his side to face the window and shifted back again to make room. Dave went to clamber on, but paused when Nicholas voiced an inarticulate protest.

"I am *not* getting naked for you," Dave insisted, interpreting this correctly. "Not here."

"You could just take off your jeans …"

"No, mate. I'm sorry, but no."

After a moment, Nicholas tipped up his chin in agreement, and Dave climbed up onto the bed, which was unnervingly higher off the floor than a regular one. He settled quite naturally with his back to Nicholas so they were spooning, with Nicholas encompassing him warm and strong just as Dave had imagined.

Nicholas shifted up on an elbow to look at Dave, and push closer still for a kiss. "There … That's sweet …" He chuckled in quiet happiness. "Remember how we used to while away whole afternoons like this, back at the waterhole, on the bonnet of the Cruiser … ?"

Dave snuffled a laugh. With the top half of the bed propped up at an angle, it was almost exactly like lying up against the Cruiser's windscreen. "Yeah, I remember …"

Nicholas didn't say anything more, but pressed a kiss to Dave's hair, to the sensitive spot by his ear, to his cheek, to his forehead – and then to his mouth. Another. And then they settled into a proper kiss, lush and gorgeous. Dave slipped his hand back to mould to Nicholas's hip, and Nicholas spread his palm and fingers and thumb against Dave's chest just over his heart, rubbed at him reassuringly and then slowly caressed his way down further and further still until he could slip his hand in under the hem of Dave's t-shirt and flatten warm against Dave's belly.

A peaceful warm hush had fallen, and they might have been anywhere. They might have been safe alone together at the waterhole – and in any case, Dave had sprung to full happy life, so that when Nicholas asked at last, "Let me?" Dave replied in roughened tones, "O' course." And then that hand slid under the waistband of his jeans and into his boxers, and there was just room enough for the palm and the inside of Nicholas's wrist to rub at Dave's eager cock while those fingers pushed tantalisingly at his balls – and it had been so long, too long. Within moments Dave's spunk was gushing forth and he voiced a quiet "Oh!" of wonder, and as the pleasure slowly started ebbing away he opened his eyes to see Nicholas gazing down at him with infinite affection.

They stayed there holding each other's gaze for a long while, with Nicholas's hand gently cradling Dave's tackle as if he loved it soft and tender as much as he did hard and rampant. Eventually Dave remarked, "Well, okay, I guess you're starting to get the hang of this."

Nicholas's mouth quirked in delight. "Excellent. Give me another seven years to practise, and who knows what I might achieve!"

"Mate, and I'd give you another seventy after that, if I could."

"Deal," said Nicholas. And he looked down at Dave with the most gorgeous smile: half besotted, half wry, full of hope, and wholly Dave's.

One thousand and three, Dave happily noted – and he pressed a smile of his own to those plump pink lips, and let his eyes convey the entire marvellous heart of the matter. *Nicholas Goring Taylor, I love you true.*

About Julie Bozza

Ordinary people are extraordinary. We can all aspire to decency, generosity, respect, honesty – and the power of love (all kinds of love!) can help us grow into our best selves.

I write stories about 'ordinary' people finding their answers in themselves and each other. I write about friends and lovers, and the families we create for ourselves. I explore the depth and the meaning, the fun and the possibilities, in 'everyday' experiences and relationships. I believe that embodying these things is how we can live our lives more fully.

Creative works help us each find our own clarity and our own joy. Readers bring their hearts and souls to reading, just as authors bring their hearts and souls to writing – and together we make a whole.

I read books, lots of books, and watch films. I admire art, and love theatre and music. I try to be an awesome partner, sister, daughter, friend. I live an engaged and examined life. And I strive to write as honestly as I can.

I have lived in two countries – England and Australia – which has helped widen my perspective, and I have travelled as well. I love learning, and have completed courses in all kinds of things. My careers have been in Human Resources, and in eLearning and training, so there has always been a focus on my fellow human beings and on understanding, conveying, sharing information.

Knitting gives me some down time and the chance to craft something with my hands. Coffee gives me stimulation and a certain street cred. My favourite colour has segued from pure blue to dark purple, and seems to be segueing again to marine blues.

I think John Keats is the best person who has ever lived.

And that's me! Julie Bozza. Quirky. Queer. Sincere.

If you want to know more, please do come find me at juliebozza.com and libra-tiger.com.

Titles by Julie Bozza

The Butterfly Hunter Trilogy:
       Butterfly Hunter
       Of Dreams and Ceremonies
       Like Leaves to a Tree
       The Thousand Smiles of Nicholas Goring

Albert J. Sterne:
       The Definitive Albert J. Sterne
       Albert J. Sterne: Future Bright, Past Imperfect

Novels and Novellas:
       The Apothecary's Garden
       The Fine Point of His Soul
       Homosapien … a fantasy about pro wrestling
       Mitch Rebecki Gets a Life
       A Night with the Knight of the Burning Pestle
       A Threefold Cord
       The 'True Love' Solution
       The Valley of the Shadow of Death

Stories and Anthologies:
       Call to Arms
       A Certain Persuasion
       An English Heaven
       No Holds Bard
       A Pride of Poppies

* 9 7 8 1 9 2 5 8 6 9 2 0 0 *